Cora's Crystal Stair

A Novel

Rita Roberts-Turner

Editing by Cara Highsmith, Highsmith Creative Services,
www.highsmithcreative.com
Cover Design by Mitchell Shea,
www.papermitchshea.com

ISBN-13: 978-0-9964996-2-0
eBook: 978-0-9964996-3-7

Printed in the United States of America
First Edition 14 13 12 11 10 / 10 9 8 7 6 5 4 3 2 1

Dedication

In loving memory of my father, "Dada,"
who believed in all of my dreams.

Cora's Crystal Stair

For you created my inmost being;
you knit me together in my mother's womb.
I praise you because I am
fearfully and wonderfully made;
your works are wonderful,
I know that full well.
My frame was not hidden from you
when I was made in the secret place,
when I was woven together
in the depths of the earth.
Your eyes saw my unformed body;
all the days ordained for me
were written in your book
before one of them came to be.

(Psalm 139: 13-16)

RITA ROBERTS-TURNER

Prologue

Welcome to life in Black Bottom, a shanty area of dilapidated one-room shotgun houses that bumped against leaning outhouses. It got its name because it sat in about the lowest point of the city—at the foot of the state capital—and was home to some of the poorest black people. Barefoot children played and scavenged for food on a mound of trash and debris that grew bigger every time the county trucks rolled through uninvited. Laughter echoed through the Bottom on Friday nights when the men who had jobs got paid.

Happy to have a little more than coins dangling in their pockets, they turned over what they had to the women who used it buy fresh fish and pinto beans. Whatever money they had left was spent on dice games and homemade whiskey, a combination that usually brought the laughter to an abrupt and violent end. A dispute over a hard fought fifty cents, a lingering glance at someone else's woman, or some other manner of alleged disrespect would be followed by an attack of empty Mason jars crashing into dirt patch yards next to still smoldering cigarette butts. But, all would be forgotten in the morning when the neighbors laughed over weak black coffee while the children collected the shiny pieces of glass and pretended they were diamonds. Children here were never planned, and sometimes not even wanted. They just happened. Cora Bell Matthews was one of those unplanned. Cora entered the world under hardship. A breach baby they called it. The midwife had to reach right inside her mother and yank her out. She didn't breathe for a whole minute; at least, that's what her father told her. And nothing but the prayers of the church ladies gathered around her mother's bed brought her to life. "Praise God!" they all shouted when she let out a faint cough. She followed her brother Bo, and next came their little sister Mae, who they just called Lil Sis.

RITA ROBERTS-TURNER

Chapter 1

Cora tied and retied the red ribbon on the end of her long braid. Covered in gold glitter with pin-sized rhinestones along the edges, it was the fanciest ribbon she'd ever seen. It was also the first brand new thing she'd ever gotten.

"You turning twelve today. You needs something as pretty as you," her mother said. She gave Lil Sis a giant rainbow swirled lollipop and Bo a white handkerchief with the letter B embroidered in black. They admired their gifts, not paying attention to the man in the oversized suit and gold front tooth standing in the doorway, until their father's booming voice erupted from the yard. Then a silver pistol appeared from the stranger's waistband. Their mother begged their father not to make a scene as she hopped into a black Cadillac and sped away.

Cora's father spent most of the first week their mother was gone in a drunken fog, staring at the door each day waiting for her to reappear. Nosey and murmuring neighbors descended on the little house, bringing cakes and pies for the children, which kept their empty bellies from rumbling at night. The first card from their mother came after a couple of weeks, with candy and a few dollars. One more card arrived offering paper kisses and letting them know she missed them. Then weeks turned into months of nothing.

"I gots me a job," Bo announced over the small plate of cornbread Cora had managed to scrape together with some cornmeal and milk she'd gathered from neighbors. Tired of hunger and waiting on their father to emerge from his emotional coma, he'd gone to the coal yard with the neighborhood men. Bo was big for only fourteen years old. The yard supervisor liked his size and youthful vigor and figured he could get the work of two men out of him for less pay. "I starts in the morning."

"What about school?" Cora asked.

"That schooling ain't gon put no food on this table," he said, looking to his father in disgusted pity as he slept off his drunk in a chair by the door.

"I'll gets me a job too," Lil Sis said with childish excitement. "I can sit with white women's babies."

"You'll do no such thing!" Cora snapped. "You're staying in school."

Cora worried that Bo would expect her to quit too. She was at that age where she could take on washing and caring for other people's babies as most of the girls in school had done.

"Teacher says we colored folks won't do any better until we get educated."

"Teacher says, teacher says," Lil Sis mocked.

"You both stay in school. I'm working."

Bo got up from the table, finished off a cup of buttermilk and took a long stretch. "Headed to bed. I gots to be a work tomorrow," he said, smiling with the pride of manhood.

Cora and Lil Sis trudged off to school, their bellies still hollow from the night before. Cora hated to see Bo stop learning, but with steady money coming in the house, there would be one less thing to worry about. Inside the bare one-room schoolhouse, children of all ages packed themselves around the wood burning stove, eagerly waiting for their hot hoe cake and syrup the teacher passed out after they dutifully said the pledge of allegiance. The warm spongy bread was the only thing that brought most of them to school, many of them slipping out after the obligatory recital of the alphabet and counting to 100. Others, including Lil Sis, made their escape at the sound of the recess bell that seemed to ring sooner every day. Cora stayed behind. Resting her chin on her hand and thumbing through the pages of a tattered textbook, wondering what important words lay between all the missing pages. Her teacher, a soft-spoken, tall, thin, pasty woman, gave her a list of words to practice writing. She had taught at the school for five years and was given a stipend by the Methodist Church when the State claimed it had no money to give to the colored schools. She took a particular liking to Cora often helping her with her sentences and insisting she speak the King's English, much to the chagrin and amusement of Cora's neighbors.

"Cora, this is my last week at the school," her teacher said as she cleared off the chalkboard and gathered up the broken bits of chalk. She'd asked for a fresh box before she left, but it was doubtful the request would be granted. She eased beside Cora on the wooden bench and handed her a book, a complete book, bound in leather, with all the pages intact.

"This book is by a colored man named W.E.B. DuBois. Have you ever heard of him?"

"No ma'am," Cora answered, not taking her eyes off the book.

She opened the jacket, slowly afraid of damaging even one page. She ran her hand across the title, *The Souls of Black Folks*. Below the title in deep black marker was a scribbling of letters, her eyes questioning the teacher.

"That would be Dr. DuBois's signature. He signed it for me and this is my gift to you."

Cora's heart pounded. She didn't have any real books at her house other than the Bible. Even the bedtime stories she told Lil Sis were all from the bits and pieces she remembered her mother telling her as a little girl. She turned each page, inspecting the words, feeling the grain of the paper between her fingers.

"You just have to promise me one thing," the teacher told her. "Don't ever stop reading or learning."

Chapter 2

The school didn't reopen. Cora wanted to keep reading and learning as she promised, but like all girls her age, it was time for work. The neighborhood women told her father it was foolishness for a grown thirteen-year-old to be sitting up in a classroom with little children when she could be bringing some money home. She found a job doing laundry for some of the housewives on the west side of the city. None seemed bothered by the fact that she was just a girl or that the weight of their heavy baskets sometimes nearly toppled her over. Five baskets a week brought in about three dollars.

She gave Lil Sis fifty cents for helping her deliver the clean clothes, a dollar went to help pay the rent and another dollar for food. She gave a nickel to the church and put the rest away for herself, not for any particular reason. Maybe she'd get an ice cream or go to a picture show if she found the time. Most nights she was too tired to do anything except count her money.

"Cora, you got five dollars saved up," an excited Lil Sis said as she sat on the edge of the bed watching Cora count. "What you gonna do with all that money?"

It was Bo's sixteenth birthday and his thick curly hair was slicked back and the little mustache above his lip was neatly trimmed—he had treated himself to a barber. Cora baked him a cake with thick homemade chocolate icing. Any other day he would have fussed at her for spending the extra money, but today he happily licked a glob of the frosting from his finger and washed it down with a Coca-Cola. For a rare moment, the house was truly joyful. Even their father made an effort to stay sober. It helped that Cora hid away his whiskey.

"Look at you, boy. Sixteen," his father said as though they had come to the satisfying end of a long journey. "Ain't no man in Black Bottom prouder than me today. This is from me and yo Lil Sis," he said, handing him a stiff white dress shirt folded into a neat square with a necktie perched on top of it and a pack of cigarettes all held together with a piece of twine. That's what Cora's five dollars had gone toward.

He reluctantly pulled an envelope from his pocket. "And this here is from yo mama."

He held it midair waiting for Bo to take it. The room was frozen. They hadn't heard from or seen their mother in two years. There were rumors and whispers about her being in Harlem. Others had said St. Louis. Bo took the envelop from his father. The return address was for Chicago. It was still sealed but crumpled. Cora was sure her father had contemplated tossing it in the trash. But it wasn't his to throw away.

"Open it, open it!" Lil Sis begged.

He ran his fingers beneath the sticky seal, careful not to rip into the address on the outside of the envelope. Two dollar bills poked out from a note inside. He read it to himself.

"I'm gonna go see mama in Chicago," is all he said before tucking the note back into the envelope and walking out of the house.

*****

Cora hadn't really expected Bo to just take off for Chicago or for him to be gone for a year, and neither did the foreman at the coal yard who got tired of asking about him and finally gave his job to somebody else. He'd written a few letters and hadn't mentioned when he was coming home, but there he was walking slowly up the yard as Cora hung out the morning wash. She ran to him and gave him an unreturned hug. He looked thin and tired as he walked past her and into the house. Without saying a word, he took down the one picture they had of their mother—a grainy black and white photo with the three of them propped on her lap—and threw it in the trash.

"What happened?" Cora asked, shocked and wanting to rescue the picture. "What did Mama say?"

"It don't matter," he said. His voice flat and almost emotionless.

Just then Lil Sis ran through the door.

"Bo is home!" she wrapped her arms around him. "Did you see mama? Did she ask about me? Is she coming home?"

"No!" Bo said, as if a switch had just been ignited. His booming voice startled Lil Sis and Cora, and they moved away from him. Seeing their fear, he took a sorrowful breath.

"Mama ain't never coming home," he said solemnly. There was no point telling them what he'd seen. The men, the drugs, the shell of a woman who didn't even resemble their mother anymore. He was surprised she'd even remembered his birthday considering the state she was in. When he found her, she introduced him to some men who were prepared to show him how to make big city money. They laughed at his overalls, but admired his muscles. "Yeah, we can use a big old country boy like this," one of them laughed. Bo remembered the gold tooth. He especially wouldn't tell them what he'd been doing in Chicago to get enough money to make his way back home.

Lil Sis started to cry and Bo put his arms around her and Cora.

"No matter what, always know that you is loved by me, you is loved by Daddy, and you is loved by God," he said solemnly looking at them both before announcing he was heading to Georgia to work on the peach farms.

Cora and Lil Sis cried and asked him what was in Georgia that wasn't in Tennessee.

"Maybe a little more money . . . and new memories," he said quietly.

Folks stood around the radio in front of the Five and Dime listening to President Truman announce the end of segregation in the military. Cora thought, as she passed a Whites Only sign, that it was odd how he saw fit to let colored men get killed along with white men, but not drink out of the same water fountain. It didn't matter to Bo. He already wrote home that he'd joined the Army. Cora didn't ask how he'd gotten enlisted at only seventeen years old. She figured he did like a lot of the boys in Black Bottom seeking a steady paycheck and the promise of seeing the world.

Lil Sis was taking in laundry with Cora, but that work was becoming sporadic as more and more women were looking for full time help. Lil Sis was still too young to do much else, but a neighboring housekeeper told Cora about a young northerner who was a newlywed and a little strange. She'd overheard her misses and her husband talking about the woman needing somebody and they asked her if she knew somebody who needed work.

RITA ROBERTS-TURNER

Cora stood at the back door of Miss Lillian's home, waiting for someone to answer her knocking. She didn't see a doorbell so she knocked again, finally getting the attention of a petite red-headed woman with a cigarette dangling from her mouth. She opened the door and looked quizzically at Cora. Her hair was pulled tightly back with a nest of curls in the front.

"Can I help you?" she asked, blowing a pillow of smoke toward the sky.

"My name is Cora; I was told you're looking for a maid."

"Ha! And who told you that?" she asked, sounding both amused and irritated. Her voice was loud and big for someone Cora guessed was barely over five feet tall.

Cora dropped her head. "Sorry ma'am. I must have the wrong house."

The woman put out her cigarette and opened the door wider.

"No you don't have the wrong house. I'm sure this is my husband's doing," she paused and curled her lips. "You might as well come in since you've come all this way."

Cora followed her inside and waited to be told to sit.

"What did you say your name was again? Cara?" she asked lighting another cigarette.

"Cora ma'am. Cora Matthews."

"Well, Cora, I'm Lillian. Do you have a car?" she quizzed.

She talked through her nose and had a funny

way of dropping the *r* in her words.

"No ma'am, but I can easily take the bus. It's stops not far from the house."

"Umm, and what would you like to do for me?"

The question caught Cora off guard. She had never been asked, only told what to do.

"I can clean, do laundry, cook. Anything you need ma'am."

"Cora there is nothing in this house that I or my husband shouldn't be able to do for ourselves. But apparently that's not the way things are down here. So, I'll ask you again, what would you like to do?"

Cora's young hands had become cracked and dry from laundry, and she hated ironing. Cleaning the large house alone would be back-breaking. If given a choice, she'd choose cooking.

"I'm a mighty fine cook ma'am."

Lillian sprang from her seat. "Very well, cook it is. You can start tomorrow. Feel free to look around," she said, rushing off to answer the telephone. Cora could hear her, ranting from the other room.

"A maid. Can you believe it, Daddy? It's like the 1800s down here, and I swear these poor Negros think they are still slaves."

Cora had a million questions, like what did she and her husband like to eat? What time should she come to work? How much would she be paid? But, for now, she was just satisfied to have a real full-time job.

Cora got up early and joined the other women at the bus stop. There were maids as young as thirteen and as old as seventy congregated together, laughing and gossiping about their white families. Cora tugged at the uniform a neighbor let her borrow until she got her first paycheck and was able to buy her own. Her hips hadn't filled out as much as the older women, but her body was definitely coming into womanhood, and Cora felt self-conscious as she tried to sit comfortably on the bus. Miss Lillian's house was the last stop on the route.

She knocked at the backdoor and waited patiently, remembering how long it had taken Miss Lillian to hear her the first time. Miss Lillian finally appeared, still in her bathrobe, her face bare and her fiery red hair falling loosely to her shoulders. She looked much younger than she had the day before.

"You certainly start the day early don't you Cora?" she said as she let out a big yawn.

"Yes ma'am," Cora said wanting to remind her that she didn't tell her what time to come to work.

"Well, the kitchen is yours. Enjoy," she said, heading back to bed.

"Um ma'am, what would you and your husband like for breakfast?"

"My husband already left for the office and I don't do breakfast," she grunted. "And one more thing, there's a front door for a reason. Unless you are a pet or a car, please use it from now on."

Cora sighed and looked around the massive kitchen unsure of what she was supposed to do. If nothing else, it was quiet and she took out the book she'd tucked away in her bag. The Souls of Black Folks, maybe one day she'd finish it as she'd promised her teacher.

Cora thawed a piece of meat, covered it in foil to roast with some tired carrots she'd found in the refrigerator. She scrounged through the kitchen and found some canned peaches, flour, and sugar, managing to pull together a cobbler just as Miss Lillian came into the kitchen around noon.

"It smells good in here," she said. "I can't believe you found something to cook."

Neither could Cora. She'd never seen such bare cabinets and a nearly empty refrigerator in a white family's home.

"I'm happy to do the grocery shopping for you ma'am if you'd make a list," Cora offered.

"Oh that's not necessary. I purposely refused to go to the store this week. I was proving a point to my husband."

"Starvation doesn't seem like much of a point ma'am," Cora said, instantly wishing she could retract her words. But oddly, Miss Lillian started to laugh. Like her voice, her laugh was big and loud. She laughed so hard that she almost made Cora loosen her guard and laugh.

"You're funny Cora! I'm going to like you," she said. "Go to the store and get what you need." She handed Cora $50 and her car keys.

Cora stood hesitantly staring at Miss Lillian.

"Let me guess, there's some southern code and you're not allowed to drive my car," she said with exasperation.

"No ma'am that's not it. I just don't know how to drive."

Lillian broke out again into even harder laughter. This time Cora joined her.

Working for Miss Lillian was easier than most jobs.

The pay was fair, and Miss Lillian always put a few extra dollars in the envelope. "Our secret," she told Cora. "My silly husband insists that all you maids are supposed to make the same. But I know how hard you work."

Most days, Miss Lillian left Cora alone to do her cooking, while she raged to someone on the telephone about her husband's archaic ways.

"If I didn't just adore that man, I would just pack a bag and head right back to Boston," Cora could hear her stomping up and down the hallway.

Cora only saw her husband, Mr. Jameson, as he expected to be called, near the end of her day when she set out their supper. He had taken on the role of deciding the evening meals. He was always polite, but they existed within the comfortable distance Cora was accustomed to.

Chapter 4

Bo was headed off to war, Lil Sis had a boyfriend and Cora was turning eighteen. It didn't seem like she'd worked for Miss Lillian for two years. She'd found her a "good white family," moving as an invisible but necessary part of the house.

In the serenity of the kitchen, she found moments to read letters from Bo, detailing as best he could, his adventures in Korea. Once the day's meal was prepped and ready for the oven, she sometimes sat with a sandwich and scribbled poems into a little note pad she'd kept from her days in school or read a few pages of her book. "This year I promise, Dr. DuBois, I'll finish you," she said to the book. But recently, Miss Lillian started insisting that Cora sit and drink a cup of afternoon tea with her.

Miss Lillian was the only woman Cora knew who found a cup of hot, barely sweetened tea to be an ideal beverage in the heavy southern summer heat. But then she was from Massachusetts, so most things about her were still odd to Cora. While they sipped tea, she spoke of how her love for her husband was the only thing that had brought her down south. She complained about the mosquitoes being too big, the iced tea being way too sweet, and racial progress being paralyzed by small minds unable to comprehend that the South lost the Civil War. She refused to join any of the ladies' social clubs and told her husband she didn't need or want a maid. But as one of the state's prominent businessmen and a Southern gentleman, he made it clear some things weren't up for negotiation. There was an image to maintain. So she hired Cora and as an act of defiance. That's why she greeted her at the front door each morning and why Cora suspected she served her afternoon tea in the dining room.

Cora didn't like hot tea, but Miss Lillian had never bothered to ask her. She was like a lot of white people Cora knew—those who wanted to be applauded for their noble gestures without concerning themselves with how black people felt or what they wanted. Every day she sat uncomfortably on one of the antique high back dining room chairs and took a few sips of the bland drink, eager to escape back into the kitchen. Usually, they enjoyed polite silence, but today Miss Lillian wanted to talk. She sat a worn notepad on the table and tapped it with her forefinger. An accusing grin spread across her face like a parent who hadn't seen her child with a hand in the cookie jar but spotted the tell-tale crumbs on her mouth.

"Cora, did you write the poems in this book?" Miss Lillian asked in an understated tone.

Cora froze, her cup still at her lips. She had forgotten to put the notepad back in her bag and must have left it in the kitchen. Everything she'd written was fiction. She hadn't been careless enough to write about the lives of white people, whose secrets were well dissected by the maids and drivers who lived in Black Bottom. Still, had Miss Lillian read something she thought was too familiar, or did she just not appreciate Cora loafing on her time?

"Well, did you?" Miss Lillian asked again somewhat impatiently.

Her mind raced, thinking of which poem Miss Lillian might have read. There were the ones about her mama and Black Bottom, and one she'd titled "Washer Girl."

Cora sat down her cup and swallowed hard.

"Yes ma'am," she said barely above a whisper. She kept her eyes fixed on the table.

"Interesting."

Miss Lillian studied Cora as if waiting for her to

say something else. Cora needed this job. Her brother wasn't able to send much money home, her Lil Sis was still too young to get real work, and her father was out of work most of the time. She would apologize. White people like that. But she wouldn't beg.

"You beg white folks for anything then you spend the rest of yo' life beggin', steppin', and fetchin'," her father warned years ago.

"I didn't mean any harm ma'am. I was just scribbling on my lunch breaks is all. It won't happen again," Cora said as humbly as she could, keeping her eyes firmly fixed on the table.

"How old are you Cora?" Miss Lillian asked, dismissing Cora's apology.

"Seventeen ma'am. I'll be eighteen this week."

"How far did you get in school?"

"Sixth grade ma'am."

"Remarkable."

Cora slowly raised her eyes, catching a quick glance at Miss Lillian's face. She seemed more intrigued than perturbed. Maybe she was slightly embarrassed that she didn't know these small details about Cora.

Miss Lillian opened the notepad and read a random page to herself. Then she looked at Cora again, almost suspiciously.

"You write this well and only have a sixth grade education?"

Cora didn't want to talk anymore, and she really had nothing else to say. She had dough to knead, pie to bake, and a ham to prepare. Mr. Jameson would be home in a few hours. He liked to see his meal on the table, but not the help behind it, when he got home.

"I should be getting back to the kitchen ma'am."

Cora collected their cups and waited for Miss Lillian to hand over the notepad. She was reading another page. Something made her smile. Cora timidly cleared her throat and held out her hand.

"I'd like to hold on to it for a little while if you don't mind," Miss Lillian said as she got up from the table. Cora's insides began to churn and feel weak.

Miss Lillian would tell her husband and he would be upset. Miss Lillian was different from him. She might find Cora's ability to put words together sensibly on a page entertaining like a state fair attraction. Her husband would not.

The next morning, Cora approached Miss Lillian's house with a hopeless dread. She hadn't called to tell her not to come in. She was the kind who would rather tell Cora in person. Cora sighed. At least it was Friday and she would get her last paycheck she thought.

Miss Lillian wasn't waiting for her as usual at the front door for all the neighbors to see. Cora went around the back of the house and quietly opened the kitchen door. Miss Lillian was sitting at the kitchen counter.

"Good morning, Cora," she said, smiling and watching her move nervously around the kitchen for an apron.

"Good morning. Would you and Mr. Jameson

like chicken for dinner tonight?"

If she could get through the day that would mean a few extra dollars before she heard the words, "You're fired."

"Cora, come sit down," Miss Lillian demanded in a way that sounded almost inviting.

"I should probably get started with the cooking ma'am. I know how Mr. Jameson likes a big Friday night supper."

"Don't worry your head about Jack right now. Come. Sit."

Miss Lillian reached under the counter and pulled out what looked like a giant square hat box. She struggled a bit to lift it and Cora figured it was filled with some old knick-knacks Miss Lillian didn't want anymore. Giving them to Cora would make her feel better about firing her.

"This is for you, Cora," she said. "Open it."

The top didn't fit perfectly onto the box and the sides were taped to keep it from falling off. She hooked her finger around the loose middle of the tape and tore it off. Inside the box were three large pads of paper, a box of No. 2 pencils, and a black typewriter with some of the finger pads missing. Miss Lillian leaned over Cora. Her head almost resting on her shoulder.

"Go on, take it out of the box, it's yours. It belonged to my father."

It was old, but Cora had never had a typewriter before. She was excited but afraid to show it, especially if this was her parting gift.

"Consider it an early birthday present," Miss Lillian said. She had a satisfied grin as if knowing she was the first to ever give Cora such a gift.

"I told Jack about your stories last night. Of course he swears you probably plagiarized them from somewhere because, in his Antebellum South mind, no colored person around here has the wit to walk straight and drink a Coca-Cola at the same time. But we know better don't we?" She playfully winked at Cora as if they shared some kind of secret Lil Sis-hood.

"I know good writing and your work is good. This is just a little something to help you keep at it."

"Thank you Miss Lillian. I don't know what to say," she finally managed to speak. "This is about the nicest present anybody ever gave me."

"Well you are very welcome. Now you must do something for me."

Here it is, Cora thought. *White people never just freely gave black people anything.*

"Yes, ma'am," Cora said dejected.

"Do something meaningful with your life," Miss Lillian's head bobbed excitedly up and down. "What do you want to do with your life Cora?"

It was the trick question white people loved to ask. They liked confirmation that black people were as happy as they could possibly be. And if they weren't, white folks were good about showing blacks just how unhappy they could make them. Like Tom Richards. Orphaned or abandoned depending on who you asked, he started working for a local white family when he was just ten years old. In exchange for a warm corner in their barn, he cut and hauled tobacco, cared for the cattle, tended the crops, and rendered any other service they needed. When the master of the house died the mistress sold the land and moved away, but she gave Tom the little shack barn that had become his home. He took money he'd saved, bought some dried goods and opened a store for the area blacks. He grew and sold his own vegetables and rolled single cigarettes from the little tobacco he harvested. He managed to buy a few dairy cows and sold milk by the cups to those who couldn't afford much more. He worked on his store day in and day out. He rebuilt the barn, painted it, and hung out a sign "Tom's General Store . . . serving all." After a while, even the poor whites were coming to his store. And before long, his little store was burned to the ground. He left the county with little more than the clothes on his back.

"That's what telling white folks yo' dreams will git ya," Cora's daddy told her.

"I suppose get married and have a family like everybody else."

"No, no, no. I mean what are your dreams? You do think about leaving this place, don't you . . . like you write about in your stories?

"No ma'am. Those are just stories. I like it here just fine with my family and working for you and Mr. Jameson."

"Well I can't let you do that. I simply cannot let you stay here and waste that mind of yours."

Mr. Jameson liked to eat his dinner in silence and read the paper. Usually, Miss Lilian obliged, but tonight she couldn't contain her excitement.

"I've decided to help Cora do something with her life," she announced.

Mr. Jameson looked up from his paper, wiped his hands on his napkins and looked quizzically at his wife.

"Who?" he asked.

"Cora . . . our cook," she said rolling her eyes. "I want to send her somewhere where she can write and think and meet people."

He sat stone still, knowing that she wasn't finished.

"A girl that smart is wasting her life here cooking your . . . our . . . meals."

He took a deliberately long bite of food.

"You see this," he said, waving his hand over the array of food. "this is what . . . what is her name again . . . Cora does. She cooks for us. That's her job and she enjoys it."

"And how do you know that?" she asked defiantly.

"Because I'm from here. I know what makes our coloreds happy. We treat her fairly, pay good wages, let her take leftover food home . . . .."

"Yippee. Well I've made some calls and I can get her a job and a place to live in Washington DC."

His face reddened.

"You will not be giving our cook my hard earned money to go on some fool trip."

"It's not a fool trip and it's not your money I'm using."

Miss Lillian's eyes widened and danced with excitement as she blurted out, "I've made some calls and arranged for you to go to Washington, DC!"

Cora's mouth slightly opened but she couldn't form any words. It didn't matter because Miss Lillian rattled on without giving her a chance to say anything. She told Cora how she contacted some people who would set Cora up with a job at Howard University. She'd be cooking for the students during the day, but at night, "There's a whole Negro world to explore and write about," Miss Lillian said, delighted by her own accomplishment.

"And you'll be staying in a Christian boarding house with other young Negro women."

Miss Lillian stood like a dog panting for a

sampling from his master's table, waiting for Cora to form her answer. She handed her a small gray envelop with Greyhound Bus written across the top.

"Sunday Cora—that's your birthday right?"

Cora nodded.

"Be on that bus and don't look back."

Cora tried to find her words. Her mind was racing. She knew the answer was no, even though deep down in her inner gut, she wanted to throw her arms around Miss Lillian and scream, "Yes! Yes! Yes!" Instead, she said as calmly as she could, "I appreciate the offer ma'am, I really do. But I have to talk it over with my Papa."

"Absolutely not!" her father shouted as he stumbled over a chair. He'd started drinking earlier than usual, even for a Friday.

"A self-respecting good Christian girl got no business running 'round in Washington, DC, by herself. I ain't gon' let you end up like yo' Mama."

Those were his last words before collapsing on the couch. Looking at him, his head bobbling and jerking as if trying unsuccessfully to wake up from a bad dream, Cora knew she had to leave.

Chapter 3

*Leave your country, your people and your father's household
and go to the land I will show you.
I will make you into a great nation and I will bless you;
I will make your name great, and you will be a blessing.*
—Genesis 12:1-2

U Street wasn't hard to find. The air was a sweet and salty mix of fried chicken and fresh baked waffles swirling with the riff of a nearby saxophone. Rows of well-dressed men and women—all of color—moved rhythmically along the sidewalk greeting each other with a polite smile or tip of a hat. Cora walked a few blocks, trying to restrain her country girl new-arrival grin.

She had money for a cab. Once her father sobered up and accepted her determination to leave, he insisted she take some "fall back" money if she was "hell bent on following some white woman's fool idea." She didn't know how he'd scraped up fifteen dollars and decided not to tell him Miss Lillian had given her fifty. He needed to feel like her father—important and a hero. She decided to hold on to the money and walk.

She liked weaving in and out of all the unfamiliar faces and being a part of the bustling DC afternoon. But the thought of having to ask for directions terrified her and she was relieved to find her destination easily.

Miss Irma's Boarding House for Christian Negro Women sat squarely between two smaller homes. The sign out front was white with black letters and two sets of brown praying hands at the top and bottom. It stretched across a partial iron gate that was ornamented with crosses along the top. The house itself was painted a deep pink and trimmed in white, which made it stand out even more from the other houses. Free-flowing ivy ran up the sides and window boxes were filled with pink, purple, and white flowers that Cora didn't realize were fake until she touched them.

She set her suitcase on the porch and rang the doorbell. She waited, her stomach bubbling both from hunger and nervous anticipation. When no one came to greet her, she rang the bell again. Finally, a stern-faced woman opened the door. She offered no hello, but looked Cora up and down with a clear and immediate air of disapproval.

"Um, good afternoon," Cora said nervously and stepped back from the door a few inches. "I'm looking for Miss Irma."

Silence.

"I have this note for her."

Cora pulled a small envelope from her purse. It held the letter of good reputation—apparently a requirement for tenancy—from Miss Lillian. There was also first month's rent. The woman took it from her hand and looked suspiciously at Cora. She slowly read the letter, her face softening only slightly.

"Follow me," she said in a tone that was more ordering than inviting.

Just inside the door was a chandelier that was catching the sunlight from the windows and forming a faint rainbow. Cora thought that had to be a good sign. Maybe a reminder from God that He was with her. To the left was a sitting room, neatly decorated with a floral sofa and two large pink chairs facing a fireplace. Miss Irma definitely favored pink and flowers, Cora noted. A radio and Bible sat on a mahogany table between the two chairs and a portrait of Jesus hovered above the mantel. The dining room was on the right. In the center of the room was an elegant table covered with a lace tablecloths and China place settings for ten. Cora gazed at the dining room in disbelief. She didn't know any black people who actually had a dining room. And, except for her tea time with Miss Lillian, she had never sat at such a grand table.

"We eat every evening at 6:00 p.m.," the woman said with a hint of impatience as she moved Cora along.

The bedrooms were upstairs. Two rooms of them side-by-side with the doors wide open. In each, Cora could see three beds, all neatly made and in a row, two dresser drawers, and a closet. There was a small vanity against the wall across from the beds with another portrait of Jesus hanging overhead. At the end of the hallway was another door shut tightly. Cora assumed that was Miss Irma's bedroom.

The woman pointed to a stripped bed and said this one was assigned to her. At the foot were linens, two pillows, and a blanket. She handed Cora a key and a list of instructions and rules.

Cora scanned the rule list.

NO MEN ALLOWED.
NO LOUD MUSIC.
NO SMOKING.
NO DRINKING.
NO LATE RENT PAYMENTS.

The list of Nos went on and on including the last rule: NO SOCIALIZING WITH THE UNIVERSITY MEN.

"These rules are very important if you want to stay here. I suggest you learn them well," the woman said as she turned to walk out the door. "And I am Miss Irma," she added matter-of-factly as she disappeared down the hallway.

With Miss Irma gone, Cora took a deep breath. She could already tell a little bit about her roommates by how their beds were decorated. One had replaced Miss Irma's standard issue wool blanket for a soft yellow spread with a ruffle at the bottom. Her side smelled of a sweet happy perfume, like lemons and vanilla. Cora inhaled. She had never smelled anything so lovely. She also had an extra pillow with a matching yellow sham. The other bed was more understated. A patch quilt tucked in at the foot of the bed. A few photos were scattered on the vanity of smiling girls wearing Sunday dresses. One had a yellowish magnolia in her hair. Cora suspected she was the roommate who smelled good.

Cora tossed her suitcase on her bed. The

ride on the bus had been long and was followed by another equally long train ride. She noticed that she smelled like moth balls and cigarettes. There was only one bathroom and, according to the rule book, each girl was allowed fifteen minutes in the morning and another fifteen minutes before bed. She decided to take advantage of being the only girl in the house and maybe sneak in an extra five minutes.

Soap, towels, and washcloths were stacked neatly on shelves with each girl's name. Cora was pleasantly surprised to find her name on the bottom shelf. She sank into the warm water, feeling the smooth porcelain against her skin. She loosened her hair and let the ends dangle on her chest as she squeezed the wet rag across her face. She lathered herself from head to toe with the bar that had been left for her, and then sank deeper into the tub to let the water lift the suds from her body. She closed her eyes, and a broad satisfied grin spread across her face. She had arrived.

She hadn't thought about the time or her

fifteen-minute limit until she heard a rush of girlish chatter coming up the stairs. The clock near the sink showed five o'clock. Cora could make out at least four voices as she hurried to dry and slip into a fresh cotton dress she'd brought. It was one of only three that she owned. Her hair had drawn up into tight coils and she pinned it back. By the time she opened the bathroom door, the voices had moved into the bedrooms. The two doors that had been opened were now closed. When she stepped into her room, two girls were stretched out on their beds rubbing their feet.

"Well, hey there," the one with the yellow spread said and sprang to her feet as soon as she saw Cora. "You must be the new girl. Cora, right? Welcome!" She pulled her into an unexpected hug and Cora got a faint smell of lemon and vanilla, mixed with the work of the day. She was the girl in the picture with the flower in her hair, although she looked much smaller in person and prettier too. Her accent was different and Cora couldn't quite make it out. It was Southern, but nothing she'd really heard before.

"I'm Elaine. Elaine DuVey," she said proudly, emphasizing her last name as if it were important or someday would be. "I'm from Nawlins."

Cora had never met anyone from New Orleans. The other girl rose more slowly and walked with a slight limp toward Cora. She extended her hand. It was rough and marked with healed over scratches, the kind Cora saw on the men at home who worked the cotton and tobacco fields.

"Name's Loretta," she said in a tired, but pleasant way. "From Miss'ippi. Let us know if you be needing anything."

Cora nodded. "Pleasure to meet you both."

Loretta got back into bed and Elaine started peeling off her work clothes. Cora felt a little embarrassed watching her stand there and undress.

"Loretta likes to take a rest before supper," Elaine said.

"I got bad legs," Loretta chimed in. "All of us

ain't on easy office duty."

Elaine rolled her eyes. "Loretta works in the university laundry. Her choice. Anyway, where are you from?"

"Tennessee," Cora answered, glancing past her to Loretta.

"So where are you working?"

"I've got a job at Howard University."

Elaine laughed. "Child, I know that. We all work at Howard. Where are you assigned?"

"In the kitchen. I'm supposed to be cooking."

Elaine leaned back on the bed and rolled down her stockings. She extended her long, lean legs and arched her foot like a dancer.

"Well, good luck, honey. I started in the kitchen too. The boys loved my gumbo," she said, proudly. "Now I'm a mail girl for one of the professors because I can read and write."

"You know that ain't why you got that job," Loretta jabbed. "That man like the way you walked."

Elaine twirled her hips and winked then darted off to the bathroom. Loretta laughed and Cora cracked a shy smile. She watched Loretta massaging her scarred legs. They looked like her hands and Cora suspected she had spent much of her life working alongside men. She had some mint oil, which she'd made herself, in her bag. She always rubbed it on her father's hands and knees when he'd come home from the fields. That and a drink always seemed to make him feel better. She wasn't sure why she'd packed it, but she offered some to Loretta.

"Try this," she said, handing her the small glass jar.

Loretta opened the lid and sniffed. She instantly recognized the smell.

"Mint oil! Just what I need. Ain't had me none of this since I left Miss'ippi," she said excitedly.

She rubbed a generous amount of the oil up and down her legs. She propped her feet up on her pillow and took a soothing breath of air.

"Thank you," she said, exhaling.

"How did you end up in the laundry room?" Cora asked.

"You got kitchen, laundry, and housekeeping. My cooking ain't nothing to shout over and I didn't want to be on my knees scrubbing floors, so I picked laundry," she said and offered Cora a mint. "And I got a plan. Gonna work my way up to head laundress and just walk around telling other folk what to do in a few years."

Elaine walked in, wrapped in a satin robe stained with water on the back. "Yes ma'am you'll be head laundress and head old maid," she shot out.

Loretta threw a peppermint at her. Elaine ducked and laughed.

"I'm just saying. No men are coming through the laundry room. Not a one." She walked over and placed her hand under Cora's chin and lifted it as she boldly inspected her.

"Now, you are a pretty girl. You should have

yourself a gentleman caller real soon, but you can't be walking around here in no one dollar dress from Tennessee."

"Don't pay her no mind," Loretta said. "Everybody up here ain't looking for no Howard man to take care of them."

"Well, they ought to be."

Meeting a Howard man—any man—wasn't of interest to Cora. There were boys back home she could have stayed and married if that's all she wanted to do. Her father often grumbled through the house that she should be married off by now. He pointed to her Lil Sis who was already courting somebody seriously, and she was just fifteen.

"I thought fooling around with the university men wasn't allowed," Cora reasoned.

"Honey, if you're planning on following every rule on Miss Irma's list you might as well crawl up under a church pew and tell the Lord to take you on to glory now."

Loretta let out an unexpected high pitch laugh and said, "Amen!"

Before she knew it, Cora was laughing too and, with that, the three roommates quickly became friends.

Cora met all the girls over a breakfast of oatmeal, one slice of bacon, and a piece of toast. Besides Cora, Elaine, and Loretta, there were three other girls: Susie, an interesting looking girl with freckles and sandy brown hair, from North Carolina, worked in housekeeping with Ethel, a tall, lanky girl, from Florida. Inez was assigned to the laundry with Loretta. Inez didn't talk as much as the other girls and never introduced herself to Cora, other than to mumble that Cora was sitting in her chair.

"Lawd have mercy Inez, we ain't got no assigned

seats," Loretta rebuked. That's how Cora learned her name. Inez stood over Cora waiting for her to get up. Cora thought about staying put, but decided it would be disrespectful with this being her first morning in the house.

"Good morning. I'm Cora," she said, offering a smile. Inez nodded and slide into the chair, barely giving Cora time to move her plate.

"Inez is not a morning person," Susie explained.

"Or afternoon or evening," Ethel chimed in.

The girls giggled and Inez shot them a cold glare. As menacing as she tried to look, Cora noticed a lonely sadness in her eyes.

The kitchen was already busy when Cora arrived. It was two hours before the breakfast hour and everyone had a station. Cora was in charge of biscuits. All the cooks were women, but the supervisor was Mr. Richmond. He had learned how to cook in Paris, France during World War II, but when he came back to the States, nobody was looking for a negro French chef. So he landed at Howard, directing the kitchen with musical precision.

Cora smoothed out her crisp white uniform, adjusted her hair net, and got to work. For two hours she cut, baked, and delivered piping hot biscuits to the dining hall, invisible to the rush of hungry students. The girls wore dresses with thin sweaters draped across their shoulders. Some of them flirted with the young men who came in with their bowties and suit coats. A few wore sweaters with a huge letter H embroidered on it. It was the end of the first week of school and everyone was comparing notes about what they'd learned, whom they'd met, and whether or not the freshmen were of any account. None offered a thank you to the staff as they moved through the food line or even gave a thought about how long people had been up so they could have a bountiful breakfast before their classes started. When they were finished eating, the cleaning crew swooped in and the kitchen staff started on lunch. Cora was responsible for rolls this time, and the scene was repeated all over again.

The bad thing about Cora's first day being on a Friday was that she wouldn't get paid like the others. The good thing was the cafeteria closed early because many of the students went home for the weekend or to a placed called The Hamptons while it was still warm. Everyone was rushing out the door and chatting about their plans for the night. But Cora had nowhere to be and she wanted to explore the campus.

After being indoors all day, the last bit of sunlight felt good. As she walked, she heard Elaine's voice calling out to her.

"You're going the wrong way. Bus stop is this way. You don't want to miss that early one," she said, walking briskly to catch up with Cora.

"I thought I'd do a little sightseeing," Cora said.

"Child you're gonna see enough of this place. Now come on. You can go dancing with me and my beau Fred. He's pre-med. I bet he can even get a friend for you," Elaine urged.

Cora politely declined. She'd seen Fisk University and Tennessee State University from a distance at home, but she'd never been on a college campus. She grabbed her things, freed her full mane from the hair net, and continued her stroll. When she found a nice oak tree in what she guessed was the middle of campus, she sat down, leaned against it, and pulled out the book she'd only gotten halfway through. She was interrupted before she even had time to turn the page.

"Well, I know now that we serve a mighty God," a powerful voice said.

She looked up to a rich coffee-colored man standing over her, blocking the sunlight. He was wearing one of the "H" embroidered sweaters and his hair was slicked back into deep waves. He had strong cheekbones that rose higher as he grinned. Cora had seen him earlier in the cafeteria laughing loudly with his friends.

"Excuse me?" she said as if she hadn't heard him correctly.

"Only a mighty God could have made a creature as beautiful as you," he went on.

Cora stared blankly at him and, without a word, turned her attention back to her book.

"That bad, huh?" he finally said, mocking himself. "I told my friend no self-respecting woman would fall for something so corny."

"Please be so kind as to let me start over. Good afternoon, I'm Thurston Edwards." He kneeled down and squatted in front of her, steadying himself with one hand and extending the other to her.

She raised her eyes to find him smiling at her. His Clark Gable-like mustache accentuated his white even teeth. He was good looking, that was for sure, and she hoped she wasn't blushing.

"Cora . . . Cora Matthews," she said, reluctantly placing the tips of her fingers in his outstretched hand and then withdrawing them almost instantly. His hand was softer than any black man's she'd ever met. She knew he hadn't done a day of hard labor in his life. His clothes were expensive too, she could tell.

He glanced down and saw t she was reading *The Souls of Black Folks*. He felt even more foolish about his failed attempt at flirtatious banter.

"Isn't that book profound?" he asked. Cora searched the dictionary in her head to remember what *profound* meant. "I mean the way Dr. DuBois just tapped into our psychological condition. I've never read anything like it." He was enthralled, genuinely excited to have a conversation with a woman on campus that was about more than the latest social club. "Are you reading it for class?"

Cora almost laughed out loud. He had no idea she was a cook. She raised herself up and he took her elbow to help steady her. She brushed off the debris and put the book back in her bag.

"No, not for a class," she said.

Thurston was finishing his final year of medical

school. Having completed his undergraduate degree at Howard, and after seven years on and around the campus, he knew most, if not all, of the upperclassmen. He hadn't seen Cora with the throng of freshman women who spent their first week on campus milling about the male-dominated medical and law schools. But she was definitely new. Her face had that naïve, excited look.

"Well, then I'm even more impressed. Truth be told, I haven't found too many enlightened young women on campus, especially not freshmen."

As Cora walked away, he stayed on her heels, still jabbering about the greatness of Dr. DuBois, the Negro struggle in America, and so on and so forth. Cora guessed he knew very little about the Negro struggle outside of the pages of a book.

"Maybe you would do me the pleasure of getting an ice cream with me and we could talk some more about the book," he said.

Cora was ready to end the tease.

"I can't. I'm tired. I've been baking biscuits and rolls all day for you and your unenlightened classmates."

He stood, looking at her dumbfounded, noticing for the first time the stiffness of her white dress and the white shoes that mimicked those of nursing students.

Cora saw her bus approaching and she darted off before either of them could say anything else, relieved there would be no awkward silence or obligatory conversation.

Cora was on her bed, stretched out on her stomach, her legs folded backward, feet dangling above her while she read. As she turned each page, she got tickled when she thought of Thurston's surprised face upon learning the cook was reading W.E.B. DuBois. She was slightly distracted by Loretta popping her gum every few seconds and humming along with the radio. But she was happy to have the company since most of the other girls were out on dates. Curfew during the week was 8:00 p.m. On Fridays it was 10:00. Every minute late cost the girls an extra dime for rent. Elaine slipped in at 9:58. She fell on Cora's bed and wrapped her arms around her shoulders. So close to her, Cora could smell liquor on her breath.

"I knew it. I knew it," she said, her words slightly slurred together as she snatched the book out of Cora's hand.

"Elaine!" Cora chastised. "What's wrong with you? Have you been drinking?" she asked just above a whisper, knowing Miss Irma would be doing room checks shortly.

"Don't worry about me. You have an admirer," she said playfully over a hiccup. "My beau Fred said his friend met a girl today who was reading some fancy book and thought she was the most beautiful girl he'd ever seen, and she turned out to be a campus cook."

She rolled over on her back and threw her arms up in the air. "Said he just has to see her again and he asked me did I know her. I knew it had to be you.

62

You're a little smarty colored girl, aren't you?"

Elaine broke into a spastic laughter. Cora and Loretta tried to hush her.

"Future Doctor Thurston Edwards likes you," she said poking Cora in the arm. "You need to go out with us next weekend." Her voice trailed off unexpectedly. She had dozed off to sleep, leaning all of her weight on Cora's shoulder.

Cora looked to Loretta for help. She sighed and grabbed Elaine's feet while Cora struggled to hold her upper body. They got her to her bed, took off her shoes and threw a blanket over her.

They heard a light knock at the door before it opened. Miss Irma scanned the room, checked her watch, and noted everyone was present.

"What should we do?" Cora asked nervously, after Miss Irma had left.

"Nothin.' She be alright in the morning, long as Miss Irma don't find out."

They turned out the lights and Cora tucked

herself comfortably under the covers, listening to Elaine's soft, drunken snore. So Thurston Edwards thought she was beautiful. Cora figured that was probably a figment of Elaine's drunken imagination, but she still fell asleep smiling.

Chapter 7

The school kitchen moved at a frantic pace on Monday mornings. Supplies arrived. Mr. Richmond was busy planning the week's menu; and, because no one had been in the kitchen all weekend, the cooks only had a few hours to prep everything for the day's meals. and an assembly line of ladies frantically chopped and diced vegetables. Another group raced back and forth from the kitchen to the dining hall, refilling trays on the steam table as a crowd of morning students started to file in. Wanting to make sure her supply of biscuits kept pace with demand, Cora peeped through a small round window of the revolving door that led from the kitchen to the steam table and waited for the server to come retrieve the tray from her. Unexpectedly, she caught a glimpse of Thurston in line for his meal.

"Don't just stand there, girl; get those biscuits out on the floor!" Mr. Richmond suddenly barked at her.

"But," she started to say.

"But, nothing," Mr. Richmond interrupted. "You see that line. Get moving."

Carrying the tray of warm biscuits, she kept her head down, hoping Thurston wouldn't notice her as she dropped them under the heat lamp.

"I think these might be the best biscuits I've ever eaten. Please give my hats off to the cook," he said deliberately loud enough for her to hear before she ducked back behind the door.

The day felt longer and harder than Cora expected.

"Monday's are always the worst," one woman

told her as they all filed out of the kitchen for the day. Making her way out of the cafeteria, Cora noticed the sun was beginning to set earlier as fall was moving in. The weather was still pleasant for walking, but she could not enjoy it. Her feet were tired and she was taken by surprise, finding Thurston standing by the steps. She attempted to pretend she didn't see him, but he slipped up beside her.

"Can I help you?" she asked trying to hide a smile.

"I'm just trying to decide," he said, looking at her.

"Trying to decide what?"

"Decide whether you are prettier with or without that hair net."

Cora shook her head and let out a slight giggle.

"You still haven't done me the honor of having ice cream with me," he said.

Cora wasn't sure whether he was serious, especially now that he knew she was a cook. But a part of her wanted to take his hand and go.

"I'm afraid my bus will be here any minute, and it's the last one of the day," she said, coming back to her senses.

"Well, you're in luck. I have a car. I can take you home."

Cora's face dropped and she gave him a suspicious glare.

"Mister I don't know you well enough at all to be getting into a car with you," she said with a huff in her voice. The bus pulled up and Cora hopped on with an air of sophistication that intrigued Thurston even more.

The next day when Cora got off work, Thurston was back waiting by the steps. This time he was holding two vanilla ice cream cones.

"My apologies," he said, handing her one of the cones. "May I walk with you?"

Cora softened and she licked the few drips of ice cream that had fallen onto her hand. "For the record, I prefer butter pecan."

Thurston laughed and said, "Duly noted."

Giant interlocking trees with dying blood orange leaves arched cat-like toward Thurston's boxy Ford as he whizzed down a long narrow stretch of road. Cora didn't know where they were headed. Elaine had simply said in a high-pitched squeak that they were all going for a drive while spritzing Cora with lemony perfume and making her try Red-No. 3 lipstick.

Thurston took a sharp turn and the car was swallowed up into the trees. He stopped in the middle of a flat field of matted grass and leaves. This was the kind of place you discovered accidentally. It was a perfect place to keep as a hideaway for secret indiscretions. As she watched Elaine and Fred disappear in the backseat, Cora wished she hadn't worn the perfume or the lipstick. She and Thurston sat in uncomfortable silence, pretending not to hear the low moans coming from the backseat. A nervous itch was moving up

Thurston's leg, but he was afraid to move. He tried to shift his weight, careful not to slide near Cora who sat with her hands tightly knotted on top of the purse resting in her lap. Thurston knew bringing Fred and Elaine along was a mistake, but he didn't think Cora would come with him alone.

"Would you like to go for a walk?" He finally asked, unable to ignore being rocked by the synchronized movements of Fred and Elaine's bodies.

"There's a big tree stump not too far. We could sit and talk."

Cora didn't look at him. She wanted to run from the car and go back to the boarding house, but she had no idea where she was. She gripped her purse tighter and nodded.

The fall air felt sharper in DC than in Tennessee and Cora felt a slight shiver come over her. Thurston offered his jacket, but she declined. The tree stump was old and desecrated with heart shaped carvings, initials, and dates that had meant something years ago to someone. It overlooked a small creek and Cora and Thurston quietly watched a few frogs playing, jumping in and out of the water.

"I'm really sorry about the situation back there," Thurston said, feeling obliged to apologize for his friend's behavior.

"Mr. Edwards," Cora started formally.

"Please just call me Thurston. You're making me feel like you're talking to my father."

"I don't know why you brought me out here or what kind of girl you think I am . . .."

"The kind of girl who obviously has more class in her little finger than all of us put together," he interrupted.

Cora looked at him cautiously. Thurston offered her a smile. Not a cocky grin that expressed pride, but a half-moon kind that promised he wasn't up to anything unscrupulous. Her shoulders loosened, but she kept a comfortable distance between them. She set her purse beside her and inhaled the crisp air.

Thurston had brought two Coca-Colas with him from the car and he gave her one.

Cora crossed her legs at the ankles and positioned herself so her back faced him.

"So what do you think about DC so far?" he asked.

"It's fine, I suppose," she said, looking over her shoulder at him. "But it's not home."

"Why did you come all the way up here to DC?"

She felt silly telling him about Miss Lillian and her plans to be the next Zora Neal Hurston, especially since she hadn't written very much of anything since coming to the city. Things were quieter at home. She had time to entertain her thoughts, at least at night when all the work was done and tired bodies had gone off to bed. But in DC people were always moving about, especially at the boarding house. Something was always happening, and no one seemed to like being alone.

"I want to make money and help out my family

back home," she said. Sensing that wasn't the whole story, he waited, not wanting to interrupt her.

"And what else?" he asked, when she offered nothing more.

"Maybe I'll cook at the White House one day." She wasn't sure where that idea had come from, but it made her feel a little more important.

"I have a feeling there's much more to you than that," he smiled at her with an encouraging wink.

Cora blushed. "Well, what about you? What do you want to do?" Cora asked.

Before he could answer, they were startled by the sudden rustling of leaves.

"There you are!" Elaine burst through the trees. Fred was behind her, playfully grabbing at her as she tried to tuck in her blouse. "We thought we'd lost you," she giggled.

Fred wrapped his arm around her neck and held a silver flask to her mouth.

"*I* wasn't looking for you, but I hope you had as

much fun as we did!" he said crassly.

Thurston stood up forcefully, his face turning brick red from his ears to his forehead. He was fuming with anger but decided this wasn't the time to unleash it. Fred was drunk. He wouldn't remember anything in the morning anyway.

"We better get going," he said firmly, softening only when he extended his hand to Cora to help her up.

Thurston stopped his car just a few blocks short of the boarding house. It felt wrong not to take them home and walk Cora to the door, but Thurston, like all the men on campus, knew Miss Irma's rules about Howard men going out with her young boarders. He didn't want to risk getting Cora and Elaine in trouble, and Elaine could use the walk to sober up a bit. Thurston walked around to the passenger door and helped Cora out.

"Will she be all right?" he asked motioning toward Elaine who was leaning on the car for balance while Fred was passed out in the backseat.

"She will," Cora said shyly. She was embarrassed for her new friend.

They stood inches from each other, unsure of what to do or say.

"Maybe we could go out again sometime," he said. "Just the two of us."

"I'd like that. I'd like that very much," Cora found herself saying.

"What do you do on Sundays?"

"Spend time with my Jesus," she said boldly.

Chapter 8

Thurston strolled coolly into the church, looking distinguished in his starched shirt and brown suit. A Bible was conspicuously tucked under his arm. He sat down next to Cora and tipped his hat, smiling as if meeting her for the first time, just in case Miss Irma was nearby. They exchanged coy glances as the pastor directed the congregation to stand for the morning hymn. Thurston's sweet and spicy cologne was as distracting as the tip of his hand that touched hers as they shared a hymnal and sang "Onward Christian Soldier." Cora was impressed that he didn't need to rely on the hymn book. She hadn't thought to ask him if he were Christian . . . or Baptist. She didn't know any colored people who were either or both.

After church, they went to U Street for lunch. Cora hadn't been to any of the city's restaurants. The menu was massive and, as she scanned the items, she did a quick mental calculation of how much money she had in her purse. She had been strict about spending her money, sending most of it home to her father and Lil Sis. Thurston ordered steak and fried potatoes. She settled on a bowl of overpriced Gumbo.

"Don't tell me you're one of those dainty eaters," Thurston teased.

"I'm not very hungry is all," she lied. "And Miss Irma always has Sunday supper on the table for us girls in the evening."

"Ah, yes, Miss Irma."

The waiter brought a plate of rolls and cornbread to the table. Cora imagined stuffing one in her mouth, but instead tore off a small corner of a roll and spread on a dab of butter.

"You know her?" she asked, self-conscious about chewing and talking.

"Everyone at Howard know about Miss Irma. She used to be a secretary for one of the deans. Rumor has it they had an affair and he promised to marry her but married someone else instead."

Even though she wanted to know more, she was afraid of looking like a gossip, so she quickly changed the subject. "This is a really nice restaurant," she observed.

"Great food too. I wish you'd ordered more than soup," he said as the waiter brought their meals to the table. "This is my treat, you know."

Cora had not wanted to make assumptions, and it was too late and too tacky to ask the waiter to see the menu again.

"The soup is just fine," she reassured. "So, you never told me what it is you want to do? Elaine said you are in medical school with her boyfriend."

"Yes, I am. I'll graduate in May. Ultimately, I want to become a doctor and open a clinic for poor colored folks in Harlem. That's where I'm from, New York."

Cora stared at him quizzically.

"What do you know about poor colored folks?"

"My family owns some tenement houses and I grew up watching residents die just because they had to choose between paying the rent and buying medicines that would have cured them or the vaccines that that could have kept them from getting sick in the first place."

She knew exactly what he was talking about; the only difference was she'd experienced these same tragedies up close and personal, not as a sympathetic observer. She'd helped mothers in Black Bottom dress the bodies of children dead from some mysterious illness, and she'd followed her father and the other men to shallow graves earmarked for destitute Negros. Even since Cora had been in DC, Lil Sis had written her twice asking for more money because their father's feet were swelling and he had a cough. Cora had secretly sent all the money her father had given her back to Lil Sis with instructions to put it away for emergencies. The picture she sent Cora of herself in a new floral print dress grinning deliriously at the man standing next to her was evidence she hadn't listened.

"That's mighty decent of you," she managed to say without sounding cynical.

Thurston cut a piece of his steak and put it on Cora's plate. "You have to at least try this, so you'll know what to order when we come back." He gave her a sly grin and she noticed he had a slight dimple on the upper part of his cheek.

Fall draped over DC like a wet gray blanket. The bitter October air cut through Cora's thin coat, and she was forced to buy a new one. Elaine suggested a fur-trimmed fashion statement from one of the downtown department stores and a matching hat.

"Cora don't let her spend up all your money on a silly coat she saw in some magazine," Loretta warned, recommending a thrift shop for something decent and practical.

"It's not just *some* magazine. It's *Ebony!*" Elaine corrected her. "It shows all the latest styles and fashions for Negros, and according to *Ebony*, this winter is all about fabulous fur and not dime store practical."

Cora had never owned a new coat. Other than the ribbon her mother gave her for her 12th birthday, everything she'd ever had was second-hand. She felt like she wanted to put something on that no one had ever worn before, but it didn't need to be fancy. She settled on a simple brown wool, ankle-length coat with black buttons that flared from the waist, and a brown velveteen clamshell hat with brown and black flowers clustered on top. The sales lady convinced her to buy a pair of earrings to complete her look. Cora stood in the mirror giggling and shyly posing like one of the ladies in Elaine's magazine.

Chapter 9

Thurston still waited for Cora after work each afternoon, but it was too cold now to sit by the oak tree and eat ice cream before her evening bus arrived. Instead, they sat in his car talking and laughing, usually over a piece of leftover pie she'd brought from the school kitchen. Whey they were done, he drove her as close to the boarding house as he could. On Sundays, he joined her at church and they had lunch together.

"You look very nice in that coat Cora," Thurston said as they walked into the restaurant. "Is that a new hat too?"

The purchase had drained all the money she'd saved, which wasn't much. For every dollar she put away, it seemed like her family always needed two. In her last letter, Lil Sis reported the dilapidated roof on their home finally fell in, leaving a gaping hole in the living room that her father had to scrape up enough money to fix because the landlord only gave him newspaper and plywood. Bo sent what money he could, but he griped in his letters to Cora that war was hell and the Army wasn't paying the Negro soldiers nearly what they had been promised. The money Miss Lillian had given her was also gone, covering two month's rent at the boarding house. But for a fleeting moment, Cora didn't care about the money. She adjusted her hat, feeling special for the first time in her life.

"Thank you for noticing," she said, smiling as Thurston took her arm and led her to a table.

"You haven't told me what you thought of the book, *The Souls of Black Folks*." he said, as he explored the menu. It was a perfunctory exercise. No matter where they ate, Thurston always got steak and potatoes and Cora chicken and waffles. Cora didn't want to admit that she hadn't finished the book after years of trying.

"It's a mighty fine book," she said, conveniently leaving out that she was only half way through it.

"Who are you reading next?" he asked, signaling the waiter that they were ready to order.

Next?, Cora wondered. When she was a child, she had dreamed about living in a world of make believe, surrounded by books. She would rise in the morning, spread her fairy wings broad like an eagle, perch herself on the highest tree and read the book she'd chosen for the day. She felt a sudden sense of sadness and failure at only owning one book, the same book her teacher had given her five years ago.

"What do you suggest?" she managed to ask.

He rattled off a list of books: *Invisible Man, Go Tell It On the Mountain, Annie Allen.*

Cora shook her head. She had to admit she had never heard of any of those books. "We didn't have much money or places to buy books like that at home," she confessed.

Thurston had forgotten she was a simple girl. Smart, but simple nonetheless, and still young, barely even a woman. He remembered pausing when she told him she was only eighteen. He felt foolish talking about books when her concern before coming to DC had probably been helping put food on her family's table.

"Cora, I'd like to take you somewhere special," he said, changing the subject. "Have you been anywhere else in DC besides the university, U Street, and church?

She pondered the question.

"You have to get out more and see the sites," he said before she could answer.

"Well, is that what you do Mr. Edwards?" she asked with a renewed playful formality. "Take women around DC and show them the sites?"

"I'm hoping I'll only be taking out one woman,"

he said flirtatiously without hesitation.

Cora made it clear, there was no skipping church on Sundays.

"Always give God His due," she admonished Thurston after he suggested they have breakfast instead of their usual lunch. He sat impatiently waiting for the final song and benediction. As soon as the pastor said, "Amen," he grabbed Cora's hand and headed for the car, afraid they'd get stopped by the host of older church ladies who had taken a liking to Cora and always managed to tie her up in conversation.

When they got to the car, Thurston didn't tell her where they were going. He simply started driving, slowing the car only when they got to Pennsylvania Avenue. Cora's mouth dropped as they sat facing the White House.

"Is that the . . .," Cora could barely speak. "Is that where the president of the United State lives?" she asked, trying to breathe through her excitement.

"That's what people say," Thurston answered, holding back a laugh. "Would you like to get closer?"

"Oh yes, I do believe I would," she squealed.

Thurston parked the car along the street, and they made their way to the iron fence that stood between the White House and the sidewalk. Cora had seen pictures, but the house looked bigger in person.

"What do you think the president is doing right now?" she asked, not taking her eyes off the White House. She reached her hand through one of the slits of the fence and held it in the air.

"It looks like you could almost touch the house!" she said with amazement. She imagined how she must look to Thurston, like an oversized child gawking through the window of a toy store. But he found joy in watching her. It had been a long time since he'd met anyone who still found wonder in seeing something for the first time.

"There's more to see," he said, taking her hand. They walked by the Capitol, the Supreme Court, the

Washington Monument, and finally on to the Lincoln Memorial, where she stood dwarfed and in awe of the giant statue of Abraham Lincoln.

"It's just beautiful," she said, taking in a breath.

"You're beautiful," he said.

Cora blushed as he leaned in to kiss her on the lips for the first time. She had never been kissed—not for real anyway. His lips were soft and her whole body felt warm, as if it were dissolving into his. She quickly pulled away, fearing the sense of sinfulness that rushed through her.

"We should be going," she said too embarrassed to look at him. He wiped his lips with his handkerchief and smiled at the blush of red she'd left behind that he'd hold on to as a keepsake.

It was late when Cora got back to the boarding house. Miss Irma's eyes followed her when she walked in. They nodded good evening to each other. Cora hadn't missed curfew so she escaped Miss Irma's scathing rebuke.

Dinner was over, but Elaine and Loretta had kept a plate hidden for her in the room. She was bursting to tell them about the day she'd spent with Thurston and all the things she'd seen. But Elaine was taking a bath and Loretta was already asleep, having gone to bed right after dinner as she always did on Sundays.

From the nightstand, Cora pulled the little notepad of poetry she'd started when she worked for Miss Lillian. She laid across her bed and scribbled a few lines of "The Kiss"—the beginning of her first poem in DC.

Chapter 10

A sprinkling of students unable to go home for the two-day Thanksgiving break milled about campus. Mr. Richmond told the kitchen staff their job was to make the students feel as much at home as possible at least until 3:00 p.m. when he was releasing the staff to go home to their own families. The kitchen was an assembly line of peelers, dicers, and stuffers as they rolled out mounds of turkey and dressing, mashed potatoes, and gravy. Cora was responsible for the pies. Mr. Richmond wanted apple and sweet potato to celebrate fall. Rolling out pie crust made her think of home. This would be her first time away from home on Thanksgiving.

Her eyes darted instinctively looking around for Thurston when she left work. She'd forgotten that he had already taken the train home to New York.

"I hate that you'll be spending Thanksgiving working," *he told her.*

"I can use the money," she said, insisting that she would be fine.

She let out a disappointed sigh and hopped on the bus back to the boarding house.

Miss Irma had cooked a feast for the ladies, knowing most of them couldn't afford the trip home or would be working. The table was set beautifully, covered with platters and bowls of turkey, ham, sweet potatoes, macaroni and cheese, and dressing. Cora guessed she'd been cooking all day in the solitude of her kitchen, where none of them ever stepped foot. They passed ornate serving platters to each other and ate ferociously, none noticing or caring that Miss Irma didn't join them. As they ate, she gathered her hat and coat and left in a big dark car that pulled in front of the house.

"Where's Miss Irma going?" Cora asked.

The ladies shrugged their shoulders, barely looking up from their plates.

"All this food and she's not joining us?"

"Never does," Inez said, stuffing a piece of cornbread in her mouth. "She goes off somewhere with somebody every Thanksgiving and she don't come back 'til late."

"And we all is thankful for that!" Ethel said, sending the rest of the table into a chorus of *amens*.

"Well, I have an announcement," Elaine said very matter-of-factly, pushing her plate aside. "And you absolutely can't say one word about it, not yet anyway."

The busyness of the table stopped, and for a moment she had their full attention.

"I think Fred is going to ask me to marry him," she said, a proud grin overtaking her entire face.

Almost without pause, everyone except Cora and Loretta burst into laughter.

"And me and Nat King Cole gon' run off to Paris, France together too. Maybe we can have us a double wedding," Susie mocked her, laughing so hard now that she was crying.

"See that's why I don't tell you girls anything. You're just so ignorant," she scoffed, masking her hurt feelings.

"Ooooh, listen to her using a big word like *ignorant*. Getting ready for yo high society husband," Susie kept needling.

"I think that's wonderful news Elaine," Cora quickly chimed in before any of the other ladies could get in a dig. She didn't like Fred, but she knew Elaine adored him. "When do you think he'll ask?"

"Yeah, when you thank he gon ask?" Inez asked sarcastically.

Elaine looked straight at Cora. "I think Christmas time. He told me the other night that he's just crazy about me. How he's never felt for any girl the way he feels about me."

Inez propped her elbows on the table, chewing her food like a cow churning cud. "Let me ask you, if he so in love with you and gon propose and such, why is you here with us for Thanksgiving and not with him?"

The ladies roared with laughter again, oblivious to the tears welling in Elaine's eyes as she excused herself from the table.

"That's enough," Loretta said with a forceful calmness. "And Inez, you just wish you had some gentleman calling after you."

The ladies settled back into eating their meal, murmuring to themselves as Cora and Loretta followed Elaine to their room. Elaine was wiping her eyes, pretending to be removing her make-up when Cora and Elaine sat beside her on the bed.

"Don't pay Inez and those other girls no mind," Loretta said.

"They're just jealous, that's all," Cora added.

Elaine squeezed each of their hands. "You're right," she said. "What do those silly girls know? You know he wanted me to meet his folks, but he said they had some very important family business to discuss."

Elaine gathered her composure and went to the mirror inspecting herself as if Fred might appear at any moment to surprise her. "I think that important business is me and my engagement ring," she said, her excitement returning. Just think, in a few months I could be walking down the aisle, marrying a doctor. You two would have to be in the wedding!"

Cora and Loretta nodded. "It would be an honor," Cora said. "Why don't you come on back downstairs and finish eating?" Elaine had barely touched her plate.

"Oh no, I've got to watch my figure so I can get in my wedding gown," Elaine boasted. "Just the smell of all that food right now makes me sick to my

stomach."

Downtown was covered in a flurry of white snowflakes that floated like feathers through the sky. Cora had seen snow before, but never this much. She'd gone with Elaine to the Greyhound bus station. Fred bought her a ticket home for Christmas and promised to join her for a few days.

"Oh, Cora, I think he wants to do the proper thing and ask my folks for my hand," she gushed, with a school girl enthusiasm that starkly contrasted with the sophistication Cora was accustomed to seeing from her. "My stomach has just been in an absolute knot for weeks."

Cora brought her a Coca-Cola to help settle her stomach. She'd joined her at the station not only to say goodbye for two weeks, but to escape Miss Irma's prying eyes. Thurston said he had an extra special treat for her before he returned home for the holidays. "Wear something nice," was the only hint he gave her. She borrowed one of Elaine's dresses. Against Elaine's advice, she strategically pinned it so as not to expose any cleavage.

Elaine's bus was called for boarding and she kissed Cora on the cheek.

"See you in a couple of weeks," she said. "Merry Christmas!"

Cora stood waving at her from the lobby until her bus pulled away. As more departing passengers hopped aboard their buses and a hurried swarm of arriving passengers rushed to greet their awaiting loved ones, she started to feel anxious. Thurston was supposed to pick her up from the bus station, but now she wondered if he would make it as the snow continued to fall. She hadn't brought money for another cab ride back to the boarding house and didn't know if a bus would be running. She searched the station and finally breathed a sigh of relief when, in the distance, she saw him brushing off the cold and walking toward her.

"We're here," Thurston announced as they pulled up to the Whitelaw Hotel. Cora heard some of the other ladies in the boarding house talk bout it being a Ritz-Carlton for Negros. She didn't move, feeling her heart beat rapidly against her chest.

"I think you'd better take me back to the boarding house," she said coldly.

Thurston stared at her, not understanding for a moment. And then he realized he'd brought her to a *hotel*. He chuckled, making Cora feel even more uncomfortable.

"I'll thank you kindly to take me back to the boarding house," she said again.

"Cora . . .," he started to say.

"Now!" she said more forcefully, keeping her gaze straight ahead.

"But Cora . . . please . . . listen. There's a restaurant, holiday decorations, and desserts inside. I thought we might take our picture with a Negro Santa. That's all . . . I promise," he explained. "You are a lady and I would never treat you as anything less than that."

She turned to look at him. Searching, with some skepticism, to assess his level of sincerity. In the four months they'd been seeing each other, he had been the perfect gentleman. Still guarded, she agreed to go inside.

The wind and snow blistered their faces as soon as they got out of the car. Thurston handed a valet his keys, took Cora's hand, and they ducked inside the hotel. The lobby smelled like pine trees and cinnamon. The warmth of the rainbow-colored Christmas lights surrounded them as they were escorted to the dining room where a large Christmas tree sat in the middle of the foyer, decorated with large gold, silver, and white balls. Fresh poinsettias surrounded the base of the tree. Cora's eyes followed the decorated branches toward the ceiling where a crystal like star was propped atop the cone-shaped evergreen.

"Peppermint?" Thurston said, offering Cora a candy stick. They sat beside the tree, waiting to be seated at a table. A waiter brought them apple cider and cookies. Another waiter carried a large box wrapped in gold paper with a red bow and gallantly gave it to Cora.

Her eyes widened. "What's this?" she asked.

"I guess you'll have to open the box and find out," Thurston said coyly.

Cora first removed the bow and set it aside. Then she slowly pulled a corner of the colorful, glistening paper, loosening the tape on one end so the box would slide out of the wrapper without ripping it. She neatly folded the paper and placed it beside the bow. When she opened the box, a smaller box was inside with an even smaller box on top of it. Puzzled, but intrigued, she held the smallest box in her hand and opened the top. Inside was a broach with a red rhinestone centerpiece surrounded by white snowflake-like crystals in the shape of a cross. She held it in the palm of her hand like a small fragile kitten she feared crushing.

"I hope you like it," Thurston said.

"I do! I do!" Cora said, still admiring it. "Would you put it on me please?"

With a sense of satisfaction over his successful choice, he obliged. She watched his strong but soft hands work the delicate clasp and rubbed her hand across his.

"You know there's more in the box," he playfully reminded her.

With child-like excitement she eagerly reached for the other box, yanking it open to reveal a small stack of books—the ones Thurston had recommended to her.

"For the start of your future library," Thurston said.

She took a breath and started to cry unexpectedly. Not a harsh, loud sad cry, but a joyful whimper. Aside from Miss Lillian funding her move to DC, no one had ever given her a gift that said, "I see you."

"I hope those are happy tears," he said, dabbing her cheeks with his handkerchief.

"Goodness gracious, I don't know what's come over me. And all that ridiculousness in the car. I'm so sorry . . . this . . . this gift is so wonderful. Thank you."

He draped his arms around her and kissed her. She usually shyly pulled back, but she didn't this time. Instead, she savored the taste of peppermint and spice on his lips.

Cora and Miss Irma were the only two in the boarding house for Christmas. The other ladies, having been working longer than Cora, had money saved to go home. Thurston stayed in town until Christmas Eve, leaving only because his mother would never forgive him if he missed her annual Christmas Eve party. He went reluctantly, saying it was an absolute bore and he'd much rather be with Cora. He promised to be back for New Year's Eve until Cora told him her festivities would include evening church service. She hoped he would surprise her and come anyway.

Miss Irma sat in the parlor listening to Christmas music and reading her Bible. She made egg nog and fruitcake and left it on the dining room table. In the morning, Cora would be joining her pastor and his family for Christmas. It seemed sad to her that Miss Irma had no one to visit and no one visiting her.

"Won't you join me?" she asked Miss Irma, inviting herself into the parlor and holding two slices of cake.

Miss Irma's eyes widened, but she offered no cheerful holiday smile.

"Please turn off the lights when you go to bed," she said, excusing herself.

"Yes ma'am," Cora said, shrugging her shoulders.

Miss Irma turned and watched Cora nibble at the fruitcake. It had been a kind gesture—one she didn't typically receive or extend.

"Cora, you're not like these other girls. Remember that," she said very matter of factly.

"Yes ma'am," she said, confused.

Sitting alone under the glow of the Christmas light Miss Irma displayed along with a few other sparse decorations, Cora read the letters from Lil Sis and Bo.

Lil Sis and her father got the chocolates and winter scarves she'd mailed. Bo estimated he'd be home by the summer if the war kept going like it was. When she was finished with the letters, she opened the box of books from Thurston. She smiled, trying to decide which one to start reading first, but she pulled out her own notepad instead. Her next poem was simply titled "Thurston."

At least thirty guests crowded into Thurston's parents' home for their annual Christmas Eve brunch. The elite crowd included his father's medical partners, the executive leadership team for his mother's social club, along with a smattering of club donors who would hold spiteful memories during the club's annual fundraiser if they felt slighted, and their parish priest who came each year to give an obligatory holiday Episcopal prayer and ensure all were in attendance for evening church service. They all milled about, eating finger foods and drinking for a polite amount of time. The closure of his father's bar was usually a sign to leave. His mother, Alice, doled out air kisses and waved goodbye to everyone except one mother and daughter pair who stood waiting dutifully in the foyer. They had been invited to stay longer and visit, with Thurston in particular.

Shuffling everyone to the living room, his mother directed the seating, forcing Thurston and Harriet to squeeze together on the loveseat.

"Harriet's people are in the banking business," she said passing coffee and cake to the two of them. Subtly wasn't an attribute of Alice embraced.

Their holiday meeting had been planned for

weeks, orchestrated mainly by Harriet's mother, Mary, who knew the value of marrying well. She had cozied up to all the women in her social club who had sons. Most were either already married, too young, or not ambitious enough. But Thurston seemed to be the right combination of everything and was expected to take over his father's sprawling Harlem medical practice someday. Mary outwitted and outworked all the mothers with single daughters who had their sights on him. She volunteered for every club committee Alice chaired, opened her home for meetings, and donated money that they really didn't have. She piqued Alice's interest when she announced Harriet would be attending Howard to study nursing. Alice had tried to keep herself out of Thurston's romantic affairs, but he was getting older and she could not leave his marital future to chance.

"Harriet's great-grandfather started one of the first Negro banks in his hometown, and her father just became a . . . vice president . . . right dear?" Alice pressed further.

"Yes ma'am," Harriet answered.

"A vice president at Industrial Bank in Washington, DC," his mother added.

"That's nice," Thurston said politely. Harriet offered a coy smile.

"With her family moving, Harriet will be attending Howard in the fall. Her mother and I thought it would be good of you to show her around campus," Alice chimed in when the conversation seemed to be coming to a premature and uncomfortable end.

"You do know Thurston will be graduating from the medical school in the Spring?" she asked Harriet.

"I'm sure she does," Thurston sarcastically interjected. Alice shot him a look, a deep frown line emerging across her brow.

Thurston's father nursed a glass of scotch amused and trying to stay out of the way of the inevitable family business merger unfolding, just as it had for him over twenty years ago.

"And what is it you'll be studying again, dear?" she asked Harriet, clearing her throat and regaining her composure.

"I'm finishing the last year of my nursing degree," Harriet reminded her.

"Ah, yes!" she said as though she'd completely forgotten. "A doctor and a nurse; that would just be lovely," she said out loud, surprising even Thurston, and he imagined the scrunched distress his mother's face would reflect if he'd blurted out that he was interested in an uneducated campus cook.

Harriet tried not to blush, taking a few polite ladylike bites of cake, the way her mother coached her when she'd gotten the invitation to meet Thurston and his family for Christmas Eve brunch.

Mary smiled victoriously to herself as Thurston's mother rambled on. She hadn't mentioned to Alice how the Depression had taken a toll on the family or that they'd come to New York for refuge and a fresh start after her husband's bank folded and that Industrial Bank was a last resort. She also hadn't told Harriet about the debt hanging over the family's head or that Howard might have to wait. But if the day worked out as she'd planned, Harriet would be long married before she ever had to put on a nurse's uniform and work.

Thurston's mother was now rambling on and he was no longer listening.

Chapter 12

It was 1953. *A new year of possibilities,* Cora thought as she stretched, rolling out of bed. The boarding house was full of activity again with all the ladies shuffling about getting ready for work. Cora already missed having the bathroom to herself as she knocked on the door reminding whoever was inside that it was time to rotate. Getting no answer but hearing the water run, she cracked the door open, and a pool of deep red water rushed to her feet, soaking her house shoes.

Cora threw the door open wider and saw Elaine slumped over the edge of the tub with a deformed coat hanger stretched between her legs.

"She's dead!" Susie shouted when she saw it, driving all the ladies and Miss Irma into the hallway.

Miss Irma rushed to the telephone, ordered the ladies to get some towels, and Cora sat next to the tub pulling and rocking Elaine trying to get her to wake up.

Within minutes, a tall black man with a ring of gray hair wrapping around his head at the temple had arrived and began moving silently between the girls who stood gaping in horror. He and Miss Irma worked silently, communicating only with their eyes. She wrapped Elaine's nude body in a blanket and he carried her down the stairs. Her faint moans indicated she was alive, but barely. Miss Irma followed the man to the door as the girls watched from the top of the steps. When she made the slow climb back upstairs, her face was strained and exhausted.

"This is what happens when you don't follow my rules," she said sharply when she reached the top step. "This is what happens when you country gals get it into your fool head that any one of those college boys thinks you're anything other than a good time." She glared at Cora. "Clean up this mess. All of you!" she ordered before going to her room and slamming the door.

When they were done mopping down the floor and cleaning the bathroom, Cora tipped to Miss Irma's door. Just as she was about to knock, she heard Miss Irma crying and calling out to Jesus to forgive Elaine and to help the girls.

No one ate breakfast. They were all late for work, but no one cared as they walked silently toward the bus stop. Before they left, Miss Irma gave them a cursory announcement that Elaine was alive and headed home to New Orleans. She would be shipping her things to her.

There he was, Thurston waiting for her as usual when she got off work. Cora walked by his car without getting in. He got out and waved, thinking maybe she hadn't seen him. Cora kept walking. He trotted toward her briskly, fighting the wind and calling to her. But she still kept walking.

"Cora," he said, finally catching up to her and reaching for her arm. "Where are you going? Don't you want a ride?"

She pulled away from him.

"Is something wrong? Talk to me."

She finally stopped and stared at him. Did he really not know what had happened? Could he really not know what Fred had done? Was Elaine not even worth mentioning?

"Elaine's gone back to New Orleans," she said. Her voice was tense.

Thurston stepped back and rubbed his hand over his hair. He wore a look of embarrassment. Maybe he didn't know Elaine had almost died on the bathroom floor, but he knew Fred had gotten her pregnant.

"I'm sorry to hear that," he said shamefully as if

he'd been a part of it.

Cora continued to walk. She picked up her pace, hoping Thurston would stay behind. But he didn't. When Thurston reached for her hand, she instinctively pulled away.

"What do you want from me, Thurston?" she finally asked with an irritated frustration.

"At the moment, just to know you're alright."

"No, what do you really want from me, a country girl from Tennessee with a sixth grade education who works in the school cafeteria?"

Thurston stood speechless, searching for the way to tell her that he saw her as so much more. Now thanks to Fred he might not get the chance.

"Goodbye, Thurston. I'm going home. I have to get up early in the morning and make biscuits for you and your friends."

He stood in the courtyard watching her walk away.

*****

As he headed back to his car, Thurston saw Fred standing in the campus courtyard flirting with a group of sorority girls. He charged toward him furiously and threw a punch that landed on the side of Fred's jaw.

"What did you do?" he shouted, raising his fist again.

Seeing this one coming, Fred instinctively threw up his forearm to block the blow and forcefully pushed Thurston away. Thurston lunged at him, but Fred quickly ducked and angled his body so that he was able to grab Thurston from behind and tussle him to the ground.

"What the hell is wrong with you?" Fred asked, trying to catch his breath and keep a firm grip on Thurston.

"Elaine," Thurston growled at him.

"What about her?" Fred asked, with a disdain in his voice that angered Thurston all over again. Thurston twisted loose and the two wrestled on the campus yard as a small crowd of students gathered to watch. Thurston pinned him to the ground, his arm pressing on his throat.

"What about her! Did you know she was pregnant?"

"I don't know anything except a girl like that has probably been with a hundred fellows," he said, gasping for air.

"You son of a . . .," Thurston said, delivering one firm punch to his mouth before releasing him.

Fred slid backward on his bottom and rested against a tree, taking in gulps of air slowly and spitting blood out on the grass.

"She's gone back home . . . in shame," Thurston said, lowering his voice.

"That's too bad, but that has nothing to do with me."

Thurston glared at him.

"Don't stand there judging me. You and I are the same Thurston."

"I would never do what you've done."

"Right. You'd rush home and tell your mother you got some little kitchen help knocked help."

Thurston hovered, preparing to hit him again. Fred through up his arms defensively.

"Let me ask you, why didn't you take Cora home to meet your folks during the holidays?"

Thurston stared at him without answering.

"Exactly," Fred said smugly. "You and I are the same whether you want to admit it or not," he said, wiping the rest of the blood from his lip.

*****

Cora hadn't expected to find Thurston waiting for her at the gate with a bouquet of flowers. They hadn't spoken in two weeks. She missed him even though she tried not to admit it to herself and she could barely mask her smile as she walked past him hoping he would know to follow her around the corner and away from Miss Irma's prying eyes.

"Seeing you is against house rules," she said, when they reached the bus stop on the next block.

He dropped the flowers to his side and held her cheek with one hand as he kissed her tenderly. "Cora, I want you to come home with me in the Spring and meet my parents," he said before kissing her again.

They walked around the block, stopping again just out of view of the boarding house.

"I would really like to walk you to the door like a proper gentleman," he said holding her hand.

"I'd like that, but I suspect I'd be homeless after Miss Irma throws me out."

"Then I'd have no choice but to marry you, I guess. How does Mrs. Thurston Edwards the third sound?"

The day would have ended perfectly if the only letter on her bed had been from the Treasury Department. Miss Irma had a habit of only giving the girls their mail on Sundays as if nothing important could happen during the days in between. She should have opened that letter first. Then she could have celebrated even if just for a little while.

We are very pleased to inform you that your test results have proven sufficient for you to advance to the next round of consideration for employment with our agency . . .

But seeing her Lil Sis's name scribbled across the top of the other envelope forced her to open that letter first.

"Papa ain't good . . .," the letter started. Cora had tried unsuccessfully to get her Lil Sis to speak and write better. She practiced the alphabet with her and read stories she'd made up at night when they were children before being forced to turn off the lights. But her Lil Sis only had an appetite for good food and boys.

"What I care 'bout all this book stuff? Ima marry me a good man one day, have lots of babies, and let him take care of all us," she declared.

Cora scanned over the elementary letter, describing how their father was incoherent and off balance and "not from drinking."

"Some days he can't get no words out his mouth,

won't eat and half the time sit right up in the chair and just go to the bathroom on hisself. Please come home soon," her Lil Sis wrote.

Cora met Thurston at the gate to the boarding house. He was surprised when she'd extended such an open invitation, especially on a weeknight. Unaware that Cora was no longer subject to the strict rules of the house, he was even more surprised when she greeted him with a girlish kiss on the cheek.

"Shall we walk?" she asked as she extended her hand to him.

The air was cold and stiff.

"We can go for a ride if you'd like. I'm parked just around the corner," Thurston offered.

"I'd rather walk," she said, hoping the stinging wind would serve as an excuse for the tears she knew would try to force their way through as soon as she told Thurston she was leaving.

They walked for a while in silence.

"Is everything okay?" he finally asked.

"I got an interview for a job with the Treasury Department," she said, trying to sound upbeat.

Thurston stopped walking and studied her face for some sign of the joy her announcement should evoked. This was good news. He'd wanted his parents to meet her and hoped to take her home over the next break. It would be so much better to present her as something other than the university cook. He gave her a hug and she could feel his chest muscles under his jacket. She had never seen him shirtless, but she imagined the muscles flexing and tightening as he held her.

"That's wonderful news! We have to celebrate."

"I don't have the job, just an interview."

"A colored woman such as yourself, getting an interview is impressive."

"Yes, I suppose so."

Then, after a long deliberate pause, she confessed, "But I won't be going for the interview."

Thurston's face was strained and confused. He knew she had very little formal education. But she was smart. Smart enough not to let an opportunity like this pass her by.

"I have to go home to Tennessee," she said, letting the words slide from her mouth. "My daddy is sick. He needs me. My family needs me. I'm leaving in the morning."

Thurston was unsure of what to say. "Will you be back?" he managed to ask.

Cora didn't answer. She hoped her homecoming wouldn't be permanent, but she knew life for her was usually just a random happening of events.

"Promise me we'll write each other...please," she said instead of answering his question. "Let me know everything that's happening so when I come back it will be like I was never gone."

For I know the plans I have for you declares the Lord, plans to prosper you and not harm you, plans to give you hope and a future.
—Jeremiah 29:11

When Cora met her Lil Sis at the bus stop, the small cantaloupe size pooch beneath her blouse explained the urgency of her letter. Cora had to care for their father. Her Lil Sis would have a husband in a few days and a baby to follow soon after. The man she'd met was a Korean War soldier, back home earlier than the rest because of an injury, now facing the reality that life for him was not going to be miraculously better. But he had a job and a house. He was also ten years older than sixteen-year-old Lil Sis, and he was feeling the stinging responsibility of having gotten the teenager in "a family way." Marriage before she got "too big" was non-negotiable. Cora and her Lil Sis walked to the house in silence, ignoring the obvious. She couldn't muster the word "congratulations." She'd wanted more for her. She'd hoped she'd be the first to go to high school and graduate.

"What happened to Papa?" Cora finally asked as they reached the porch.

"Don't rightly know," Lil Sis said. "He was shaking real bad one night, then all of a sudden his eyes just roll back in his head." Lil Sis's voice started to crack, and Cora was afraid to open the door. When she did, she saw him sitting by the window as if gazing into eternity.

"Papa," she spoke gently, trying to mask the horror of his frailty. His mouth was contorted and frozen. She smiled at him and he blinked as if letting her know he was there, somewhere behind that blank stare. She lifted him up from the urine soaked chair and almost tumbled under his dead weight.

"He too heavy to lift. When my man come home, he can get him up," Lil Sis said obliviously.

A flash of rage and frustration came over Cora.

Dear Thurston,

My Papa had a stroke. How no one realized it is beyond me. We finally got a doctor to come to the house. Please pray for his speedy recovery. My apologies for such a short first letter. I am sure you can imagine how hectic things are here. My Lil Sis is about to get married and we are expecting my brother's arrival home from Korea any day now. I do hope to hear from you soon.

Love,
Cora.

Cora sat in the middle of the floor by the wash basin, surrounded by the stench of her father's clothes and soiled sheets. It would be easier to throw everything out, she thought, as she dropped the sheets in the sudsy water. Lil Sis circled around her with a slight waddle, eating a piece of cold cornbread.

"How'd you let him get like this?" Cora asked,

scrubbing the sheets angrily across the washboard.

Lil Sis hung her head and shrugged her shoulders.

"And what about this situation?" Cora's condemning eyes glared as she nodded toward her swollen belly, forcing Lil Sis to hug her stomach as if shielding the unborn child from her piercing stare.

"Don't say nothin' to Papa," she pleaded in a hushed tone.

Enraged, Cora yanked her cold and wrinkled hands out of the cloudy gray water and grabbed Lil Sis's chin, dripping water down her dress.

"Don't say nothing to Papa?" she gritted through her teeth. "Papa don't even know who or where he is thanks to you!"

She gathered up all the dirty clothes scattered around her on the floor and threw them outside, hitting a small pack of stray dogs that had been scrounging for food. She doused them with the wash basin of water, sending them yelping down the street.

"And thanks to you," she turned coldly to Lil Sis, "I'm back here in this hell hole!" She went to her room and slammed the door, shaking the fragile frame of the house. Cora could hear Lil Sis crying through the paper thin walls and she immediately regretted her outburst. Lil Sis was still just a girl and scared herself. Cora should apologize . . . and she would. But not tonight.

The doctor came to the house once a week, looked Cora's father over before saying, "Not much change," and holding out his hand for his three dollars. Thurston's letters proved more valuable. He sent Cora pictures of exercises, a list of healthy foods to buy if she could find them, and a bottle of white pills. She was to give her father one every day at breakfast.

For weeks, Cora's day started the same: lifting her father's heavy body, sitting him on a pan to relieve himself, then washing him and putting him into some fresh clothes. She talked to him while she brushed his teeth and combed his hair, unsure of whether his paused blinks on an otherwise blank stare meant he understood anything. Just as Thurston had instructed her, she used hot towels to massage his feet and legs, waved his arms above his head in five minute intervals, and placed a peppermint on his tongue, which usually just landed on his shirt in a small pool of drool. At night as she put him to bed, and she prayed over him.

God I know you can heal Papa. Whatever you tell me to do, I will do. Just heal him. Make him better. In Jesus' name amen.

*****

Dear Thurston,

Forgive me for not writing as much as I would like. I am so tired at night that my eyes drift shut as soon as my head hits the pillow. To most people Papa seems about the same, but some days I think I see a little light in his eyes. I keep praying and waiting on God.

I also had a dream that you were Papa's doctor and you were here by my side. If only it hadn't been a dream. I will write again soon. I promise.

Love,
Cora

*****

My dearest Cora,

I cannot imagine your heartache right now, watching your father suffer. But like you, I remain hopeful that he will recover. I know your faith is strong. I miss you and our Sundays together more than you can imagine.

Love,
Thurston

*****

Lil Sis's wedding was a simple affair. Cora baked her cake and their father sat, strapped in a chair, with an emotionless stare as the pastor pronounced Lil Sis and Frank husband and wife. Watching them share their first marital kiss, a brief sadness swept over Cora. She mourned the premature end of Lil Sis's childhood and wondered when she would again feel Thurston's lips pressed against hers.

After the cake and well-wishes, they set off to moving her things into the house Frank had rented just a few doors down. There was no money or need for a honeymoon. Lil Sis rapidly rattled off orders for Frank to move this, pack that, put those down. He raced around trying to follow her directions and finally dropped a box on his foot. He howled out a series of unintelligible curse words and hopped around like a one-legged rabbit.

There was a laugh. A slow mellow laugh, like someone breathing deeply into a hollow log. The room stopped except for Cora's father, who sat there, looking at them and laughing.

Dear Thurston,

Papa laughed! It was so wonderful. It scared us all to death at first, but it was the most wonderful sound. He's eating better and moved his hand a little. I can't thank you enough for the exercises and the pills.

Love,
Cora

*****

Thurston's Valentine's Day gift to Cora was simple. A card, a box of chocolates, and more instructions to help her father. He would have called, but she didn't have a phone. He felt a pang of guilt as he dropped the

134

items in the mail on his way to pick up Harriet. His mother had volunteered him as Harriet's escort for the social club's annual Valentine's ball and fundraiser. This year Ossie Davis and Ruby Dee would be hosting and there would be an extra special surprise musical guest. It was so much of a surprise that his mother wouldn't even share the name with him and his father.

"But you'll want a lovely girl on your arm to dance the night away with," she gushed.

And Harriet did look lovely. Stunning really, in a floor length red velvet gown that hung off the shoulder, revealing a long lean chocolate cream neckline. He helped her with her fur wrap—it was fake; he could tell—as they took their seats in the ballroom. She fiddled with the corsage Thurston had placed on her wrist. His mother bought it, insisting that he put it on her; although it seemed like a childish high school accessory.

"Would you like a drink?" he asked.

"A martini would be lovely," she said.

Cora didn't drink, and Harriet's request reminded him of just how young Cora was.

The lights in the ballroom began to dim, and Thurston's mother stood under a spotlight on an elevated stage, flanked by her husband. After a few eloquent welcome remarks, reminders of the importance of this event to fund programs for the city's poor Negro youth, she gave a lively introduction to the house band as the stage curtain opened dramatically. After a few gracious bows, an elegantly dressed singer dove into Ella Fitzgerald-like rhythmic and jazzy scats, moving the crowd from their seats.

Harriet looked longingly at Thurston, ready to dance. He didn't think Cora danced. Harriet finally tugged gently at his arm, and he granted their request. They found a spot among the crowd. They threw their arms out, clapped, and he twirled her around twice. On the second twirl, she rebounded closer to him and gave him a quick unexpected peck on the lips. The suddenness of it caught Thurston off guard and instinctively he pulled back. Aware of what she'd done, she deflected her eyes to the floor.

"I'm so sorry. I don't know what came over me," she explained, catching her breath. "It must be the martini. I usually don't drink."

"It's fine, really," he said, feeling both amused and flattered. He imagined Cora running from the ballroom horrified if she'd done such a thing.

The dinner bell chimed and the band promised the crowd a second set after dinner. Thurston and Harriet were joined at their table by their parents. Their mothers exchanged satisfied grins. They had seen the two of them dancing and they had seen the kiss.

*****

Cora's father needed a wheelchair, draining the last of the money she had saved. He was able to scoot his feet back and forth and say a few words. Cora's days were now filled with tending to her father's needs, exercising and feeding him, and laundering the church choir and baptismal robes to be picked up on early Sunday mornings. This was a task usually done by the pastor's wife, but she farmed it out to Cora as a godly deed, knowing she needed the money.

*****

Dear Cora,

It is hard to believe that in two months I will be graduating and starting my career as a doctor. I have been given the privilege of doing my residency in New York. I wish to see you before I graduate, but I suspect that is impossible. Hoping your father continues to improve and that you are doing well.

Love,
Thurston

*****

Bo was home, arriving with a shipload of soldiers who had been honorably discharged now that victory in Korea was certain. For the first few weeks, he rose early in the morning before the house was awake and usually returned late at night, slumped to his room, grumbling, "War is hell," before shutting the door. And then one morning, he startled Cora, sitting in the kitchen feeding their father eggs and giving her a

138

boisterous, "Good morning!"

"I got a job!" he continued, wiping bits of egg from their father's chin. "I'm heading to Detroit, Michigan, to work at the Ford plant."

And just like that, Cora knew there would be no going back to Washington, DC. Not for a while. Maybe not ever. She let the idea of writing Thurston with the news run through her mind, but it settled as pointless. Whatever she imagined with him was only a dream, a dream that had come to an inevitable end.

Black and brown soldiers from all over the city descended on Jefferson Street. The war had ended months ago with nationwide festivities mainly for the returning white soldiers. The NAACP decided to honor their own, and they marched along the street in full uniform behind a festively dressed band, waving at the families and business owners who'd stood in the open doorways shouting and clapping. Women and teenage girls stood on the side of the street waiving flowers at them, hoping to get noticed.

Cora was there with Lil Sis, officially celebrating Bo's safe return, both from Korea and from Detroit, where he'd been the last two months training to put automobiles together. Robert Earl spotted her as he walked by. They'd grown up together. She was a few years younger and, except for maybe on Sunday mornings, he hadn't paid much attention to her. He and his Black Bottom boys sat in the ally, eating bologna and crackers, rolling dice, and laughing as the skinny girls with homemade dresses and Bibles in tow walked by like ducklings under the watchful eyes of the church ladies leading them to Sunday school. The boys usually received a whack on the head and a warning to straighten up and fly right. Along the way, he'd clearly missed Cora's burgeoning womanhood. Not breaking formation, he kept Cora in his sight, making his way over to her when the processional broke off.

"Cora Bell, the church girl! Look at you all grown up," he said playfully inspecting her. She looked past him, searching for her brother who had already been hustled away by a few female admirers.

"Are those flowers for me?"

"They're for my brother," she said dismissively.

"Well then, I guess you need to come on over here and have some barbecue with me if you didn't bring me any flowers."

"And why would I do that?"

"To thank me for my service to God and country," he boasted.

"I'm sure there are plenty of girls around here who'd like to go eat barbecue with you."

"But I ain't asking them," he said, flashing a smile.

Chapter 14

Robert Earl slid his arm around Cora's shoulder as they sat in the colored section of the movie house. He pulled her closer to him and started to move his hand up her thigh. She pushed it away. He tried again and she slapped her purse across his knuckles. Rejected, he shook off the burn and resolved to watch the movie. When it was over, he walked her home in virtual silence.

They had been going out for a month and she hadn't so much as allowed him to kiss her on the cheek.

"Cora Bell, you like me or not?" he finally asked, just before reaching her house.

"Why do you ask?" She was being coy. She had halted his advances on numerous occasions and was amused by how sensitive he was suddenly being. She didn't know he and his buddies had been talking. They bet him he'd never get a girl like, "Cora Bell the church girl," no matter how smooth he talked. He had brazenly declared she'd be his in a week.

"Look here, I'm not the type of man to waste my time on someone who ain't interested in me. There's a whole lot of other girls I could be spending my hard-earned money on," he said bluntly, hoping the prospect of him walking away would goad her into some sort of confession of affection.

"Girls like Annie Lee and Ola Mae Johnson," she snapped back. "I heard you took them to the movies last week."

Robert Earl ran his hands across his fuzzy hair.

Her sassiness is what had kept him pursuing her all this time, but he hated the prying eyes and loose lips of Black Bottom and longed for the anonymity being overseas had afforded him.

"Aww now, Cora, those girls don't mean nothing," he said with a put on innocence. "It's you I like."

"Well, I'm not the kind of woman to let some man who's not my husband grope all over me," she asserted.

"So I got to marry you just to get one little kiss?" he teased.

"Nope. You don't have to do any such thing because I'm going back to Washington, DC, as soon as I get some money saved up," she said, folding her arms tightly as she glared at him.

"Is that so?"

"That *is* so. So you can just go off and find some little harlot to follow you around like you're something good to eat because I . . ."

Robert Earl grabbed her face gently in his hands and planted a long, passionate kiss on her lips. Her body stiffened and instinctively started to pull away, but he held her tighter until her felt her loosen and slowly wrap her arms around his neck as she surrendered to the kiss.

"Naw, you ain't going back to no DC. You gone stay here and be my wife," he said with a satisfied grin before leaning in for another kiss.

Black Bottom manly, that's how Cora would describe Robert Earl. He was strong and resourceful. He came to the house every morning and night to help Cora with her father. On Sundays he brought crates of vegetables from the farm truck and bartered for dinner by sharing a warm cobbler his mother had made. He'd kick off his shoes, rub his stomach when he was good and full, and pull at Cora to sit on his lap, knowing she wouldn't. Not in front of her father.

When he asked her to marry him, there were

no other choices really. He piled his things into her father's house and the three of them settled in together.

At night they enjoyed supper by the radio. After getting her father securely tucked into bed and the house was quiet, Robert Earl cuddled up next to Cora. Married only one month, Cora still tensed when he climbed into bed and started pawing at her. Impatient and frustrated by her lack of experience, he usually forced himself on her until she gave in.

Then he'd go to the porch and smoke a cigarette, leaving Cora alone to sleep and occasionally dream about Thurston, wondering whether nights with him would have felt more gentle and loving.

At the first peek of sunlight, Robert Earl would get her father dressed and sit him by the window in his room while Cora made breakfast. It was the same thing every morning. Eggs, bacon, and grits. And every morning, Cora took a cup of coffee to her father, sat with him and watched the day burst through the clouds while his grits cooled. This was the routine until the morning she found her father with his head cocked in the ridge of his shoulder. He was smiling, and Cora thought maybe he was dreaming. It was only when she poked him and felt his cool forehead that she realized he was dead. She cried softly, not overwhelmed by grief and she expected. Her pastor always said death was peaceful, and looking at her father, she knew he was asleep with God. His tired body getting the rest he needed.

A week after the funeral, Robert Earl's coming home wasn't as predictable. Many nights Cora left a plate of food out for him before going to bed, only to wake in the morning to find it untouched on the table. When he did slide in after sunup, he gave her a quick peck on the cheek, changed clothes, and headed to work with no explanation of his whereabouts. When she got angry and screamed at him, he brought her flowers and acted as if nothing was wrong.

"Cora, I'm just having a few drinks with the men after work. You got to let a man be a man," he'd say.

The house was lonely except on days Lil Sis came by, toting her baby, and reminiscing about the childhood antics she, Cora, and Bo shared. There was an occasional letter from Bo. He'd bought a house and a car and invited Cora and Lil Sis to visit him in Detroit. There were no more letters from Thurston.

"Frank and me talking 'bout having another baby," Lil Sis said as she scrounged the kitchen for something to eat, seemingly oblivious to the fact that the baby on her hip was still in diapers. She cut into a piece of watermelon and gave a piece to her son, letting him chew on the rind to sooth his swollen gums. Lil Sis cooed at him adoringly, looking like she could eat him alive.

"When you and Robert Earl gonna make some babies?" she asked Cora.

Cora bit the bottom of her lip, burying the disappointment and pain of her marriage, knowing

Robert Earl was tired—bored really—with her already. She tried to talk to him about things, the way she and Thurston had during their Sunday afternoon strolls. He didn't care about much that was on her mind, and although he promised to go to church more often once they got married, something of more importance always seemed to come up when she prodded him to get out of bed and get dressed. The only thing she could count on was that he would work and bring food home, and for so many women in Black Bottom, that's all that seemed to matter.

*****

Thick pillows of snow hid the steps to Cora's front porch and weighed down the already weakened roof. She had pleaded with Robert Earl to stop by the coal yard when the first few flakes started to fall. She sent him out with two dollars and instructions to hurry back. As usual, he took a detour, and Cora was left shivering through the night as the frigid air whispered between the cracks of the house. That was the night the baby arrived.

The two women—the mistress and the wife—stood silently inspecting each other. The petite, big-busted woman looked tired and frail, but Cora could tell she was probably pretty at one time, before having her beauty drained by a man who would never really love her. She looked sullen as she handed Cora a thick patch work quilt with a sleeping baby tucked inside. They needed no words. The baby's smooth milk chocolate skin and gray eyes said all that needed to be said. She stood for a minute, watching Cora with the squirming child and thought she might take the bundle back. Instead, she backed away from the porch and disappeared under the icy moonlit sky.

"Who is this?" Robert Earl asked, when he finally returned home, a trail of perfume and cigarette smoke following him into the house.

"I've named her Roberta," Cora said with a cold and calculated sharpness. She affectionately rubbed the baby's thick curls while looking past Robert Earl.

"You need to get some milk . . . and coal for the fire."

The neighbors murmured about the playful baby girl with a head full of ribbons always draped over Cora's shoulder.

"My little Roberta," she cooed so often that people finally stopped questioning where the child had come from. Robert Earl had taken to calling her "Ladybug." Only he knew why. The new talk became about how closely Robert Earl was sticking to home, holding Cora's hand as they walked down the dusty road toward their house and bringing her wildflowers and bushels of turnip greens. Life was good for a while—long enough for her to end up pregnant with RJ.

Chapter 15

Disappointment was etched across Miss Lillian's face when Cora came knocking on her door with a full belly and Roberta hoisted on her hip, asking for her old job back. Miss Lillian didn't really need her. She had a maid and a house man now. But the pitifulness of Cora's silently pleading eyes wouldn't let her turn the girl away. And Cora was still the best cook she'd ever had. So she brought her on to cook three days a week until RJ was born. She took two weeks off to nurse him, and then left him and Roberta with her Lil Sis while she went back to work for Miss Lillian full-time. Robert Earl reverted to coming in and out of the house as he pleased, and Cora had pretty much stopped caring.

Cora stood in Miss Lillian's kitchen, rolling out biscuit dough and catching a cool breeze through the open window. Saturday afternoon was Miss Lillian's social club meeting. She sat in the kitchen with Cora, fidgeted over her silverware, and blew delicate swirls of cigarette smoke in the air. The kitchen was the only place she smoked. Anywhere else in the house would be undignified. It was curious how a lot of things mattered to Miss Lillian that hadn't a few years ago. Cora now used the side entrance and there were no more afternoon tea breaks—only a good morning pat on the arm and passing of the to-do list.

"Cora, do you still write poems?" Miss Lillian asked out of the blue.

Cora looked up from her biscuit dough. The question caught her by surprise.

"It's been a while, ma'am."

"Hmm. A shame," Miss Lillian said, looking past her and out the window as a delivery truck pulled up the driveway. She rushed out of the kitchen, summoning the maid to get the door and swearing she'd have the driver's hide if he rolled over her flower bed.

The first Saturday of the month was free clinic day. Half of Black Bottom lined up at the door by 7:00 a.m., hoping to be the first seen and to avoid the afternoon ire of the overworked and underpaid staff who seemed to resent them just for being poor. There was a separate entrance for White patients and a small side door for the few who crept out with a brown paper sack of pills to treat their unmentionable diseases—the kind ungodly men and woman passed to one another.

Mostly mothers sat in the waiting room huddled together with their children, long overdue for physicals or the removal of an aching, rotting tooth.

Roberta was stretched sleepily across Cora's

lap. Cora stroked her warm forehead. She never seemed to be fully well. RJ, with all of his toddler energy stood on his chair with arms outstretched and repeatedly jumped to the floor, testing whether he could fly. Sensing the judgmental stares of the other mothers, she pooped him on the leg, forcing him to begrudgingly sit still.

Outdated magazines and black newspapers were scattered about on a small table beside Cora, including *The Chicago Defender*, as if anybody should care what was happening hundreds of miles away. But the headline, "Negro Doctors Make Significant Donation to Community Clinics," drew her attention, mainly the photograph of Thurston in a tuxedo flanked by other elegantly dressed men and women. He and a woman stood together smiling and holding an oversized check. "Dr. and Mrs. Thurston Edwards along with other prominent New York doctors host successful fundraiser for the city's Negro community clinics" the caption read.

So he was married now too, Cora thought as she set down the paper and let out a thoughtful sigh, her mind briefly wondering what might have been if things had been different. Roberta had dozed off to sleep, and RJ was back to jumping off his chair. Cora let him be.

*****

"I love you as much as I hate you," Cora whispered to herself as she stood over Robert Earl, watching his bare chest rise and fall effortlessly under the covers. She pretended not to hear him when he stumbled in at 2:00 a.m., peeled off his clothes, and fell into bed beside her. He'd brought the stench of his exploits to their bed, just as he had the syphilis the doctor told her she was carrying. His disapproving and judging eyes looking her up and down as he gave her some medicine.

Cora's hand gripped the silver handle of the small pistol as she raised it slightly. She had never fired a gun and she braced herself for the popping sound she expected to hear . . . if she pulled the trigger. And why wouldn't she? Her finger inched around the trigger and she raised the pistol a little higher. There were six bullets and she wanted them all to count . . . if she pulled the trigger. But why wouldn't she?

She closed her eyes, took a deep breath, prayed, and began counting.

"One . . . two . . . three . . ."

"Mama, my tum tum hurt," RJ's small voice suddenly called out from the other side of the door.

Cora warned him to stop eating the candy Miss Lillian sent home for him and Roberta. She smacked his hand real good when she caught him pulling out another long strand of licorice. Tears welled up and before he could make a sound, Cora slid him a piece of butterscotch.

"Last one," she said as firmly as her soft heart for him would let her be.

She gazed at the door and back to Robert Earl. He hadn't moved. If he'd opened his eyes at that very moment, he would have been too drunk to get out of bed, let alone run away. He probably wouldn't even know what had hit him . . . if she pulled the trigger.

"*Mama,*" RJ moaned again.

Cora loosened her grip on the pistol and backed away from the bed. She removed the bullets and put the gun back in Robert Earl's sock drawer. When she opened the door, RJ was curled up on the floor, whimpering. Cora scooped up his tiny body, and he rested his head on her shoulder.

"Let's get you some seltzer water. Mama will make everything all better."

For all have sinned and fall short of the glory of God.
—Romans 3:23

Miss Lillian searched the kitchen cabinets and rattled off a list of things she needed Cora to get from the store. Cora nodded and said she'd grab them on her way to work.

"It's too much to carry on the bus. Take my car," Miss Lillian instructed.

Cora stood silently and stared sheepishly at her.

"Please don't tell me you still don't know how to drive," Miss Lillian said, sounding exasperated. She handed Cora her keys and marched her out to the car.

"Today, you start learning," she said forcefully.

But after an hour of Cora hitting her mailbox twice, rolling over her tulips, and repeatedly mistaking the gas pedal for the break, Miss Lillian decided driving wasn't for Cora. She drove her downtown herself.

"Cora, you know this is ridiculous," Miss Lillian said during the drive. "A grown woman such as yourself needs to be able to drive a car."

"Yes ma'am," Cora said, although it didn't make a bit of difference to her. They only had a beat up old truck that Robert Earl took to his hauling job every day. On Sundays she and the children walked to church. Occasionally, Robert Earl loaded them all up for a Saturday drive. Anywhere else Cora needed to go, she could take the bus. Other than running errands for Miss Lillian, Cora had no reason to drive.

"I'll pick you up in thirty minutes," Miss Lillian said, pulling in front of the grocery store. Cora would get the groceries while Miss Lillian shopped for a hat.

Cora trudged inside the store and exchanged pleasantries with the other housekeepers completing their grocery shopping duties. Their white or grey uniforms assured a certain level of courtesy that didn't always extend to the other Black shoppers, and a gentleman in the aisle in front of Cora expressed his displeasure over the disparity.

"I need a box of chocolates and a case of soda," he demanded in a rich baritone voice unlike those she was used to hearing.

"I'll get to you when I can," the stock boy said, dismissively continuing to stack cans on a shelf.

"I've been standing here for ten minutes. I'd like it now."

Like all the black women Cora knew who felt an instinctive duty to protect their black men, especially those who didn't seem to know better, she reached for the man's arm to calm him down and avoid an unnecessary wrath. When he turned around, she was speechless as she and Thurston stood face to face.

"Cora?!" he said in disbelief, almost forgetting to breathe.

Cora stepped back, her heart racing as she looked at him. Before she could fully regain her composure, he grabbed her and hugged her tightly.

"Is it really you? It can't be you? What are you doing here?

"I live here," she said, provoking an unexpected laugh between the two of them. "What are *you* doing here?"

"A convention. At Hubbard Hospital," he stammered, still in disbelief. "I was just trying to get a snack for my meeting," he said. Remembering the stock boy, he glared at him. Cora pulled him to the next aisle.

"Don't pay that any mind," she said.

"You look wonderful," they both said in unison, laughing again.

"I should have looked you up when I got into town," Thurston finally said, hanging his head. He had been to Nashville only twice. Cora had crossed his mind often, but so much time had passed between them that looking for her when he arrived seemed fruitless.

"You wouldn't have found me," Cora said. Black Bottom wasn't exactly a tourists' destination.

"I could have tried."

Thurston took Cora's hand and smiled, not wanting to let go of the moment. But Cora had to go. She hadn't finished shopping and Miss Lillian would be picking her up soon. She took her hand away.

"I'm working," she said, unloading her items onto the counter. "May I also have a box of chocolates and a case of Coca-Cola please?" she asked the attendant as she gave Thurston an approving nod.

He walked outside with her. "I'm in town for a few days. I'd love to see you," he said sincerely. "I have meetings all day today, but maybe . . ."

Miss Lillian pulled up in the car. Thurston helped Cora load the groceries into the backseat and tipped his hat to Miss Lillian. He always forgot how things were in the South.

"I have a phone now," Cora said just above a whisper. "You may call me if you like." Neither of them had paper. Thurston pulled out a pen from inside his jacket and discretely wrote down her number in the palm of his hand.

"Well who was that distinguished looking man?" Miss Lillian asked. As much as she had seemed to change, Miss Lillian had not developed the talent other White people had for looking through black people as if they were invisible. And Thurston was hard not to see.

"Just someone from the store who offered to help me with the groceries," Cora said, trying to brush it off.

"Good thing Robert Earl's not here, or I suppose he'd be jealous to death," Miss Lillian teased.

Cora blushed.

Cora sat shyly next to Thurston, nervously pinching together the ends of the collar on her blouse until her neck disappeared under the cottony ruffles. She only had two good blouses—one for serving Miss Lillian's guests and the other for serving the Lord on Sunday morning. Neither was right for the Club Del Morocco. The walls of the club were lined with photographs of a few faces she recognized from records Robert Earl had wasted his money on or borrowed from a friend, even though she forbade him to listen to the devil's music in the house with the children.

Everything around her moved to an orchestrated rhythm. Brisk tambourine-like shakes of the bartender invited the piano man to join in and stir bodies, twisting and jerking to the dance floor. In between, an energetic host grabbed the microphone and promised to take everybody higher and to a better place for the night. It was blasphemous. It was also hypnotic. Watching men in crisp starched shirts and ties laughing and lighting cigarettes hanging on the lips of women with freshly pressed up-dos. The flirtatious chatter between these teachers, doctors, and lawyers was riddled with more substance than she heard at the nameless, dim, and sweaty juke joints she had pulled Robert Earl from in the middle of the night before he could spend all the rent on weak drinks and cheap women. But behind the show of sophistication, she was still at a club. She'd heard about Club Morocco and other night spots that came to life along the city's infamous Jefferson Street in Sunday sermons warning about the weekend trappings of the devil. She wondered who Thurston had thought she'd become over the last ten years that he'd bring her here. She tugged at her collar again, straightening and re-straightening it.

He watched her for a bit from the corner of his eye. Still absolutely beautiful, he thought certain for a moment that he'd said it out loud when she glanced nervously at him. And still a good church girl.

"I shouldn't have brought you here," Thurston finally said apologetically. "We can leave if you'd like."

She wanted to scream, "Yes! Let's leave." But where would they go? To her house under the spying eyes of Black Bottom for day old biscuits and stale coffee? They would sit on hard second-hand vinyl furniture with the night air seeping through her cardboard and newspaper curtains while they talked about the good old days at Howard?

"This is fine." She lied with a robotic smile.

"I'm staying at a friend's house near Meharry. We can go there if you'd prefer," Thurston again offered, with the half-cocked smile she remembered from when they first met.

It was his last night in town—maybe his last visit to Nashville. If this was her final time seeing him, she wanted a better memory than Club Del Morocco.

"I suppose that will be fine," she finally said.

The house mimicked several others with brightly painted fencing outlining a neatly trimmed yard and a path lined with seasonal flowers leading to the front door. A warm and watchful porch light welcomed evening visitors up the short walkway. Thurston pulled into the carport. He and Cora sat still and listened to a chorus of crickets singing in the moonlight. A firefly landed on his windshield, watching them and refusing to move. Cora suddenly felt as exposed as she had in the nightclub, unsure of what her next move should be.

"My friend is a dentist," Thurston said, breaking the silence. "He's away at a conference so we'll have the house to ourselves. Shall we?" he asked, extending his hand and motioning toward the house.

"I never got to tell you congratulations on graduating and becoming a doctor and everything," Cora said as if she hadn't heard his invitation. "You've done quite well for yourself. Of course I knew that you would." She glanced at him sheepishly and then looked away.

"Thank you. I still haven't opened that clinic, but one day I will," he said withdrawing his hand and overlooking the awkwardness. "You know I've always wanted to help people—poor people."

"I remember," Cora said. She gazed out passenger the car window, imagining life on this side of the city and what the families inside the other houses were doing. Maybe couples were having drinks by the fireplace, playing a game of cards with friends, or settling down to read to their children. Whatever might be happening inside, she was sure no one was pacing the floors, wondering how they would make ends meet tomorrow.

"So what about you?" Thurston chimed in, interrupting her thoughts.

"Me?" Cora asked, perplexed by the absurdity of the question. He had seen her in the grocery store in her maid's uniform. There was nothing remotely exceptional happening in her life except maybe the children.

"I have a son, Robert," she hesitated. Saying his name made her think of Robert Earl and the impropriety of sitting in a car under the cover of darkness with Thurston. "My son RJ is in the second grade. He just won the class spelling bee. He's such a smart boy. Already talking about going to college one day. And my daughter, she's just ten years old and a voice as strong as Mahalia Jackson. She really gets the church going. You should see her. Everybody says I ought to put her in a local radio talent show but I don't know."

Cora was talking so quickly now that her mind wasn't able to process the words actually coming out of her mouth. All she could hear was the internal instruction to *Just keep talking, just keep talking.*

"I don't want her getting caught up in worldly..."

Thurston playfully placed his index finger to her lips, giving her a chance to catch her breath.

"But how are *you*?" he asked more pointedly.

How was she? No one had asked that in a long time, at least not anyone expecting a real answer. Was there any certain way to say your husband cheats on you with anything female, you're raising his love child who seems to always be sick, you spend your days aimlessly working as a cook, and before your head hits the pillow each night you ask God to give you something, no matter how small, to make you smile in the morning.

How was she? The question throbbed in her head forcing up a scream that wouldn't come out. And she started to cry. Without hesitation, Thurston moved closer and put his arm around her. Her head fell effortlessly on his shoulder and she released tea decade of tears that had been sitting on the surface waiting for just the right moment to escape. He held her tightly as her body shook loose all the weight of life she'd been carrying. Finally, she exhaled one long extended breath and found her lips next to his. Then they went inside the house.

The grandfather clock Miss Lillian gave Cora for her birthday announced 11:00 when she walked in the house.

"Sorry I'm so late," Cora said, as she rushed into

the house. She'd insisted Thurston drop her off at the bus stop two doors down from the house. Unwilling to let her walk alone at night, he turned off his headlights and slowly trailed her only shooting past once he watched her disappear behind her door. "I don't know where the time went." Are the children in bed?"

Lil Sis's eyes followed the loosened top button on Cora's blouse.

"I doubled up the yougins in the beds. No use wakin' 'em up this time a night," she said. "Figured it'd be okay for me to sleep in the room with you with Robert Earl gone and all."

"That'll be fine," she said. She had hoped to be alone with her thoughts in the quiet still of the house. But she couldn't ask Lil Sis to drag her four sleepy children out of bed and walk back to their house in the middle of the night, especially after breaking her promise to be home by 9:00 at the latest.

Cora poured herself a glass of water and drank slowly as Lil Sis continued her inspection. She was

174

a master at detecting small things the average eye might overlook, a gift she developed over the course of her own marriage. For instance, Cora's hair was still pinned into a neat French roll, but the rose bobby pin had switched from the left to the right.

"Must a been some party Miss Lillian had," Lil Sis remarked. "Hope she paid you some good overtime."

Cora let out a slight cough as if the water had gone down the wrong way. She'd forgotten she'd told her Miss Lillian wanted her to serve at an evening cocktail party.

"It's late. Let me get you one of my nightgowns so we can go to bed," Cora said, not wanting to spend the rest of the evening growing that lie.

Robert Earl's aftershave assaulted Cora's nose. She opened her eyes to find him hovering over her holding a handful of tired daisies. He'd been in Memphis for two weeks working on the railcars. According to his letters, he had two more weeks to go. The sun was just starting to creep its way into the house. Cora rubbed away the sleep and searched the room for Lil Sis.

"I sent her and the children home," he whispered, leaning in to give her a kiss. He tossed the flowers on the nightstand as he slid into bed.

"I missed you woman," he said, pulling her closer to him and moving his hand under her nightgown. The prickly stubble of his unshaven face scratched her skin as he roughly buried his face into her chest. Until ten hours ago, Robert Earl was the only man she'd been with. Now she knew what it felt like to be softly caressed, to be held without a demanding waiting on the other end, to be patiently and warmly kissed. Cora closed her eyes and wondered if any hint of Thurston lingered like the kind Robert Earl always brought home to her after a night of carousing with his other women. She waited for it to be over and for Robert Earl to fall asleep like he always did. She stared at the ceiling, listening to his grizzly bear snore. Her mind took inventory of what she'd done. Lying in bed longing for a man she could never have and lying to the one she was with. She hadn't hurt Robert Earl, only herself. She closed her eyes tightly. "God please forgive me," she whispered.

The phone jolted Robert Earl from his sleep.

"Who's calling this early in the morning?" he grumbled, reaching over Cora's empty side of the bed. "Hello," he said, his voice still gravely.

Silence.

"Hello," he said again, louder this time only to hear a sudden click.

Saturday mornings meant pancakes, RJ's favorite, and he was already on his second plate as Robert Earl sat down, joining him and Roberta for breakfast.

"Who was that on the phone?" Cora asked, keeping her eyes on the pancakes and eggs she had working at the same time.

"Wrong number I s'pose. Cora I tell you they got all kinds of jobs for colored folks in Memphis," he said, smiling as he spread out $200 across the table. "We might ought to move down there."

Cora gave him a surprised look until she realized he wasn't serious. He winked at her as she put a scoop of scrambled eggs on his plate.

"We got Mr. Ray's rent money right here," he said, laying aside a few twenty dollar bills. "All caught up so he shouldn't be coming 'round here with that fake, gold-tooth smile, bothering us for a while." Cora managed a smile. She hadn't seen Robert Earl this happy in a long time.

"Now the real question is what should I do with all the rest of this money? Maybe get somebody a new spelling book? he teased RJ, who was on his third plate of pancakes.

"And a new truck!" RJ said excitedly through a mouthful of pancakes.

"And a new truck," Robert Earl agreed, wrapping

his arm lovingly around RJ's neck.

"And what would my little ladybug like?"

Roberta starred glassy-eyed at her plate and gave Robert Earl a half smile.

"Still not feeling good?" He put her in his lap and pressed her warm face to his. The spring morning was sunny and warm, but Roberta shivered in his arms.

"Can't seem to break that fever all the way," Cora chimed in. "I took her to the clinic, but the doctor didn't say much more than last time, just let it run its course."

Robert Earl stroked her cheek. "Daddy's gonna get you a new doll. I bet that'll make my ladybug feel better." He carried her into her room and tucked the patchy quilt around her.

Cora was already clearing the table when he returned to the kitchen. He crept behind her, lifted her slightly off the floor and twirled her in his arms.

"And what about you Miss Cora, what can I get

you?"

"Put me down," she laughed, hitting him on the shoulder with her damp dish rag. RJ laughed out loud.

"I'm going to get you one of those fancy dresses like we saw downtown," he said, letting her go. "And then we'll go out to one of those fancy clubs on Jefferson Street so I can show you off."

Her body stiffened and she swallowed hard, suddenly feeling suffocated by a heavy invisible fog of shame. She went back to wiping off the table, trying desperately to catch a stray crumb that only she could see.

Last night with Thurston did not happen. Last night with Thurston did not happen, she told herself over and over again.

*****

Thurston tossed and turned restlessly all night, the scent of fresh citrus and baby powder still lingering on the sheets from Cora. He'd begged her to stay the night, just to hold each other together and talk. It had been a long time since he'd had someone to talk to who understood and appreciated his dreams. But waking up beside him under the revealing eyes of the daylight was too much for her. Still he wanted, needed, to talk to her before he left for the airport. He hoped to see her and say goodbye as he reached for the phone. Robert Earl's voice on the other end was an unwelcome surprise. He paused, deciding whether to casually ask to speak to Cora. "Hello," he heard again, before deciding to hang up. He barely got the receiver down before it rang. He grabbed it quickly. Maybe Cora sensed it was him and was calling back.

"Morning honey," Harriet said through a heavy yawn. "I tried to wait for your call last night, but I feel dead asleep."

Thurston took a breath. He had forgotten to call and say goodnight.

"I had dinner with friends I hadn't seen in a while. Time just got away from us," he managed to say.

Harriet rambled on for a few minutes about new drapes, having their parents over for Sunday dinner, and a party invitation.

"That's all fine," he said with an air of indifference. "I've got to get ready to head to the airport."

"Okay. See you when you get home . . . and be careful. I just hate you being down there in the south all by yourself. I see all these horrible stories."

"I will. I'll be home soon."

"Love you," she said.

"Love you, too," he said, the words getting caught in his throat.

Chapter 17

For I know the thoughts that I think toward you, says the Lord, thoughts of peace and not of evil, to give you a future and a hope.
—Jeremiah 29:11

Cool spring nights had surrendered to the thick mugginess of summer. It had been two months since that night with Thurston, a night Cora only thought about now during her prayers of repentance. Those prayers were growing stronger now since Roberta's last visit to the doctor.

It was a visiting resident student who had come into the waiting room looking defeated. Unlike the others before him, he hadn't shuffled Cora out the door with nothing more than a brown bag of vitamins or Cod Liver Oil. He ordered tests, tests Cora told him in advance that she couldn't afford. He assured her there was no charge before disappearing with a vial of Roberta's blood.

The waiting room was filling with other sick children and their parents. Some obviously only had colds and they filed out quickly with a free bag of medicine. Others looked frail and sick like Roberta, and were ushered into examination rooms. At least two hours passed before the doctor returned and called them into a smaller room with three chairs. The distressed look on his face told Cora he knew what was wrong and that there was no miracle he could perform. He placed his hand on Cora's shoulder.

"It's sickle cell anemia. I'm really surprised she's lived so long without real medical care. I'm sorry, but all we can do now is keep her comfortable." He left them alone in the room, giving Cora as much time as she needed to process the sting of his words. Cora had prayed for it not to be cancer. She supposed she should have given God a bigger list of things not to impose on the child. She took her home, hoping for a miracle while waiting for the inevitable. In the evenings, she washed Roberta's face, climbed into bed next to her, and snuggled with her until she fell asleep. RJ peeped into the room occasionally and would ease on the bed, resting his head on Cora too as she sang to them both. Then, one night, it finally happened. Before Roberta closed her eyes for good, she stroked Cora's face with her soft young hands and whispered, "Thank you, Mama," as if knowing Cora had done more than love her. She had saved her, at least for a little while.

At the funeral, Robert Earl sat stoically, trying to mask the guilt of knowing he'd brought Roberta into this world to suffer. He refused to look at the body and Cora didn't have the strength or desire to comfort him. She greeted guests as they piled into the church with their heads down, paying their respects.

Church mothers, smelling like fried chicken and potato salad, filled the seats along the outer aisles, waiting with fans in case anyone was overtaken by the

Spirit. The deacons, all friends of Robert Earl, stood prepared to open the service in song and prayer. They would drink later if that's what he needed. Miss Lillian came too, carrying a massive bouquet of flowers. She walked them right up to the altar and delicately placed them across the casket before wrapping her arms tightly around Cora. She admonished her to take off as much time as she needed and slipped an envelope of money into her hands, giving no thought to the fact that she had already paid for the funeral.

When the service ended, Cora, Robert Earl, and RJ lined up behind the casket and began the long walk out of the church to the waiting hearse. That's when Cora saw her—a shadow of a woman weeping quietly to herself on the back pew. Their eyes met just as they had ten years ago, and they shared a knowing, silent nod as Cora continued down the aisle, trying to ignore the slight wave of movement dancing across the inside of her belly.

*****

Harriet climbed in bed and threw the covers over her shoulders without so much as a good night, still reeling from an argument she and Thurston had over dinner. All he had to do was compliment her casserole even if he didn't like squash. He never had, which Harriet didn't know. But Cora did. For the past three months, he attempted to numb his mind of any memory of her. At first, she ran through his thoughts every day. Other times he was able to push her to the back of his mind, thinking of her only on Sundays and remembering their walks together in DC. Occasionally, a song on the radio took him back to that night they spent together in Nashville, wrapped in each other's arms and thinking of no one but themselves. But usually it didn't take anything special to make him long for her. He was thinking of her when he told Harriet she was being childish for pouting just because he didn't want any of the squash casserole she'd spent all day making. He instantly wanted to take back his words and swallow a forkful when tears welled in her eyes, but then she started yelling, grabbed the dish and threw the entire thing in the trash.

"From now on Doctor Edwards, you can fix your own supper," she sobbed, and then ran up the stairs.

Thurston started to follow her, but he was unsure of what to say. He was guarded in everything now, even afraid to sleep too sounding lest his murmuring dreams revealed his betrayal. He should be gentler to her; he knew that. Cora didn't need her hand held through life or constant reassurances of her value. Cora was a survivor, and Harriet's frailty irritated him. Lately, he thought about leaving Harriet—folding up his practice and heading to Tennessee to free Cora from the hell he witnessed around her. He rationalized that it would free Harriet to find the kind of love she needed and deserved as well. But there was Mason and now the new baby to come.

He lay in bed, mindlessly flipping through the newspaper while Harriet tossed and turned. Barely, three months pregnant, she was still adjusting to a ballooning stomach again, and wrestling with their son Mason, who was asserting his two-year old independence in the worst way, had left her back aching.

"Could you rub my back, dear?" she asked softly, the traces of her anger having vanished.

He put the newspaper aside and pressed the palm of his hands into her lower back, making small circular motions until he could feel her muscles loosen under the pressure. Thurston watched her as a relaxed smile eased across her face and she dozed back to sleep. There was no leaving her, and he determined not to let Cora drift back into his mind.

*****

A convoy of bulldozers rattled through Black Bottom, striking down the last few houses like bowling pins. Cora exhaled heavily as the place that had served as the backdrop for the story of her life was reduced to oversized match sticks.

Lil Sis had left months ago, signing up for the

brand new public housing units the first day a man in a blue suit knocked on doors and showed pictures of colored children swimming in a neighborhood pool and women baking pies in their well-lit kitchen with new appliances. Robert Earl hadn't been as impressed. Even though grief had settled into every corner of the house, he refused to let the government tell them where and how to live.

"If the City is giving us colored folks anything, you better believe there's a catch," he scoffed. "They probably found gold or oil under the ground and gotta get us out so the fat cats downtown can make some more money."

Every week, the man in the blue suit knocked on doors and signed up a new family. And every week, Robert Earl shut the door in his face, leaving Cora to sit on the porch and listen to the excited chatter of wives planning how they would decorate their new homes while their husbands hauled whatever was worth salvaging to waiting cars and pickup trucks. They were one of about a half dozen families still scrambling to get their things moved now that the city had grown impatient. In two hours, Black Bottom would be a soon forgotten memory, and she'd be settled into the house Robert Earl found just a block away from the housing development where, for the first time in her life, she'd be stepping out the front door onto a plush green yard instead of a rock and glass riddled dust patch.

RJ and a few other children chased behind the bulldozers, climbing on rubble and playing their version of war. Their rowdy childhood squeals reminded Cora that there had been some good times in Black Bottom—Friday night fish fries, Saturday card games and checkers tournaments, summer church tent revivals where homemade ice cream was passed around to well-behaved children.

Rubbing her oversized belly, she was thankful this baby would never know the place that also held all of her sorrows, but deep down she wished for a more ceremonious end, some way to say goodbye properly to the cooks, maids, field hands, factory workers, mothers, fathers, husbands, wives, and lovers. She hoped somebody would always remember that they had been here.

"You ready, Cora?" Robert Earl asked, grabbing the last of their boxes.

"Ready as I'll ever be I suppose," she answered, taken one last look as the bulldozer rounded the corner.

Robert Earl stood inside the hospital waiting room, pacing and smoking a cigarette. RJ was reading, or at least trying to read, *The Souls of Black Folks* while they waited for news. The book was too old for him, but Cora had pulled it out of her long forgotten box of books and given it to him around the same time that he insisted on wearing a necktie to school each day. Cora had tried to introduce Robert Earl to the book when they first met. Instead of reading, he kissed her, and that was that. Robert Earl was dismayed as he watched RJ pour over the pages, trying to make sense of the sociological expose. He'd make sure they tossed around a football or baseball or something when they left the hospital.

"It's a girl!" Lil Sis bolted through the doors, grinning. "And a big girl at that."

RJ jumped up and tossed the book to the floor. "Can we see mama?" he asked circling Lil Sis like a high energy puppy welcoming home its owner.

"As soon as they get her and the baby cleaned up," Lil Sis said, laughing at the boyish exuberance that exposed him as still just a child himself.

She touched Robert Earl's shoulder. "She's beautiful, and Cora is good."

Robert Earl put out his cigarette and let out a quiet sigh of relief. Not so much at news that he had a new daughter. Truth be told, after Roberta's death, he didn't really want any more babies. Cora's timid announcement just days after the funeral had left him feeling numb. Maybe he was just around more, but this baby seemed to take more out of her than RJ had.

She was sick all the time. During the last month, her feet swelled up like two watermelons and the doctor made her stay in bed. And he had been at the hospital for fifteen hours, waiting for the child to arrive. His relief was that Cora was alright.

He and RJ tipped into the room. Another patient was visiting with her family closest to the door, and they had to politely scoot past them to get to Cora and the waiting baby.

"Go say hello to your baby sister," Robert Earl said, gently pushing his son toward the bed, while he kept a distance. All he could see were locks of brown curls beneath the tightly wound blanket. RJ inched closer, careful not to wake her.

"I thought we could name her Memphis," Cora said.

"Peculiar name for a girl child don't you think?"

"Peculiar name for a child period if you ask me," Lil Sis chimed in from the corner of the room.

"I figure she was made when you got back from

Memphis . . ."

"Eww!" RJ shrieked and started laughing.

Robert Earl playfully hit him in the back of the head.

"I guess Memphis will be alright," he conceded.

Memphis bounced around RJ like a tick on a dog, her pig tailed shadow always close behind his. He'd taken to calling her Tag, short for tag along.

"No Tag, you can't go to the movies with me," he said every time he had a date with some new girl. But Memphis usually whined and pouted herself right into the theater, perched in between them, holding the popcorn the three of them would share. When he played baseball, she positioned herself in the dugout, handing out the bats to his teammates and cheering for RJ to make a homerun. Their only real time apart was during school, and she had cried and stomped at the bus stop her first day when she realized she was going to kindergarten and not high school with RJ. She'd almost caused a few fights too, offering RJ up to do battle with a classmate's older brother after they argued on the playground about who had the best brother.

"I told her you can whip her stupid old brother any day," she boasted.

He endured her antics because he loved her, of course. But he also didn't want to be harsh with her, especially since it seemed like that was the only way their father knew how to be.

"If I were a boy, Daddy would like me more," she lamented one day, covered from head to toe in brick-red dust from the city's baseball field where she'd challenged a boy to a race around the diamond. They circled third base within inches of each other. Then he leaned his body into her, knocking her off balance before he raced across home plate laughing. Nearly a foot taller than the boy, Memphis charged at him and pummeled him to the ground. They rolled around in the dirt until RJ broke them up.

"Girls can't go around acting like that," he chastised her as they walked toward the ice cream shop. Ice cream always made her feel better. "And Daddy likes you just fine."

But even RJ knew there was a strange bridge of separation between them, one that Memphis tried unsuccessfully to cross. She feigned interest in cars, standing by his side with a wrench or pliers whenever Robert Earl ducked his head under the hood of his beat up but reliable pick-up truck, only to hear him grunt an order for her to place the objects on the ground. Sometimes she'd sit under his feet by the television and watch football, but as soon as she asked a question, he shooed her off to Cora. RJ supposed her presence was a painful reminder of Roberta, although the two of them looked nothing alike. A few times he'd studied Memphis, wondering which side of the family she took after.

"I got an A+ on my science homework!" Memphis proudly announced at the dinner table.

She excitedly waved the paper around for Cora, Robert Earl, and RJ to see.

"Alright! Gimme five, little sister," RJ said, laughing.

"Don't be waving papers around the table while we trying to eat," Robert Earl grumbled.

"I have the highest grade in the whole class, and I might get a trophy during school assembly," she announced, disregarding Robert Earl's comment as she often did.

"Well, we'll have to get you a pretty dress then," Cora said, affirming the importance of the occasion.

"And shoes too?" she asked excitedly.

Cora smiled, "We'll see . . ."

"Ain't no we'll see," Robert Earl interjected. "We don't have money to waste on no shoes and a dress. She got enough in the closet now," he barked.

Memphis slouched in her chair, folded her arms, and looked sideways at Robert Earl. Cora gave her a chastising stare.

"Eat your food. We can talk about this later," she said.

RJ crossed his eyes and pursed his lips together like a goldfish, forcing the still sulking Memphis to laugh, prompting her to talk some more.

"My teacher says if I keep making good grades I can be a doctor one day," she said in between smacks of chicken.

"I think your teacher needs to stop putting fool ideas in your head," Robert Earl said suddenly.

"It's no more fool idea that RJ going to law school," Memphis snapped back. RJ chuckled under his breath. She had a mouth on her to be only eight years old, and an odd sense of her own self-worth that RJ admired even if it did drive their father crazy.

"You see that, Cora. You just gon let this little

girl sass talk like that?" Robert Earl said. He angrily slid back his chair and gruffly stood up from the table, hovering over Memphis. Even when she deserved it, Robert Earl couldn't bring himself to give her a good swat on the behind. He always left that to Cora. He walked out onto the porch, letting the screen door slam shut.

"I wasn't sass talking," Memphis muttered.

"Hush, child," Cora huffed and followed behind Robert Earl.

They stood quietly, listening to the crickets just starting to sing as night was falling over the sky. A few fireflies flew pass, revealing a mosquito that was attempting to land on Cora's hand.

"You got to teach that girl some humility," Robert Earl said as he lit a cigarette.

"Why?" Cora asked, swatting at the mosquito.

"Why? 'Cause she got too many dreams this world ain't gon let a colored girl have. She needs to know that now." He took a long drag on his cigarette.

"So, you want me to tell her to plan to be a cook or housekeeper like me for the rest of her life?"

Robert Earl hunched his shoulders and looked away.

"Okay then, well, while I'm at it, I'll tell RJ he can forget about ever going to college or being a lawyer someday."

"That's different, Cora, and you know it," he said, irritation rising in his voice. "You ever seen one girl come out of here and go to medical school?"

"She could be the first," Cora said softly. "And even if it never comes true, she's eight years old. She deserves the right to dream."

Cora patted Robert Earl on the arm and headed back into the house. She looked sadly at him. He had never wanted too much of anything.

"And you ain't got it so bad," he mumbled after Cora as she went into the house.

His mother was a housekeeper. His grandmother was a housekeeper. *They never complained,* he thought as he put out his cigarette. He couldn't explain to Cora why he felt what he felt. He didn't understand it himself. Every father wanted to be his little girl's hero, but deep down he knew he wasn't that to Memphis. Why couldn't she just play with dolls and dream of marriage and babies like all the other girls? Why did she have to be different and remind him at every turn that what he had to offer her was not enough?

*****

Madison playfully pounded on Thurston like a kitten tussling over a ball of yarn. She was growing so quickly and getting heavier as she leaped into his arms. She was just eight years old and already nearly as tall as her brother, Mason. He used to greet Thurston at the door with the same high energy, but recently he'd decided he was too old for such a display of affection.

"Hey Dad," Mason said nonchalantly, bobbing his head and giving Thurston a half hug when he walked over to the table where he was doing his homework.

"Tell me a story, Daddy," Madison demanded.

"Well, what story do you want to hear?"

Harriet rolled her eyes and pulled Madison from him, purposely ignoring her whining.

"Not tonight, Madison. It's late," she said, shooting Thurston a scolding but loving glance.

"You're mother's right. Tomorrow, I promise."

He watched her march up the stairs stomping and sulking, and he regretted that he had only a few minutes to give her and Mason before their bedtime. He hoped he would be able to keep his promise. He poured himself a drink, eased onto the sofa, and loosened his tie. It had been a long night of pleading for money over bland chicken dinners, but his exhaustion didn't compare to the exhilaration of being within a few thousand dollars of fulfilling his dream of opening a clinic for the poor.

"You look tired," Harriet said as she cuddled up next to him. She'd slipped into her robe, but was still in full make-up.

"I'm okay. We had some real high dollar donors

tonight. The clinic is within reach."

"That's nice dear. Maybe you can finally stop all this running around. Honestly, I don't understand why you're killing yourself for this." She pulled her hair back and secured it with a bobby pin, then rested her head on Thurston's shoulder.

"You know I read Dr. King is starting some kind of poor people's movement now. I think he ought to stop while he's ahead."

Thurston rubbed his temple, always annoyed by her naïve rants. She had never been poor. Not really. On rare occasions she talked about the family's difficulties when her father lost his job, but she had never felt the pains of hunger or the degradation of waiting in line like cattle for a block of cheese and bag of flour. She'd never worked from sunup to sundown just to make enough money to pay the boss for letting you work his land. She didn't know what it was like to have to choose between food and medicine.

"If Dr. King can do for America's poor what he

did for us Negroes, I think he'll be the next president of the United States," Thurston said.

"Ha! Now that's just fool talk," she said, barely able to control her laughter. "You and I both know that will never happen!"

Thurston shifted himself off the sofa, loosening Harriet's grip. He knew there was no point in talking anymore. He'd grown tired of trying.

*****

Memphis fidgeted in the kitchen, eager for Cora to finish up Miss Lillian's dinner salad. She'd challenged one of the neighborhood boys to a race and wanted to get home before the sun went down so she could prove to him that girls could run just as fast as boys. Her scraped knees, scars from endless such challenges, dangled restlessly from the high kitchen stool.

"How come you have to do everything for Miss Lillian?" she asked impatiently.

"I work for her, that's why."

"Well she should make her own stupid old

salad," she whined.

Cora's jaw set firmly. She pulled her lips tightly into her face until the corners of her mouth curled upward, driving her nostrils wider. Memphis knew she had talked to much. "Here it comes" she said to herself, bracing for the sting of Cora's hand across her mouth. Just as Cora moved in toward her, they both jumped, startled by sudden tapping on the kitchen door. It was RJ. Memphis let out a quiet sigh of relief and instantly climbed down from the stool to let him in. She wrapped her arms around his waist and swung herself from side to side as though he were her dance partner. He almost tripped when he tried to take a step forward.

"Alright, kiddo, good to see you, too," he laughed. "You act like you haven't seen me in a month of Sundays. I was at the breakfast table this morning."

RJ finally broke her grip and leaned over to give Cora a kiss on the cheek.

"Boy what are you doing here?" she asked. "I've

got a few more things to finish before I'll be leaving. You want to take your Lil Sis home with you?"

Memphis nodded eagerly and then quietly fell back into her chair as Cora's glare reminded her that she was one word away from getting that smack.

"I got a letter today," he said, handing over a white envelope with his name on it.

"A letter." Cora heard nothing else.

The room went still and quiet, and she could feel her heart beating through her blouse. One by one, the boys in Black Bottom kept getting letters directing them to report for duty. Vietnam was calling on them to be heroes. She held the letter in her hand without looking at it. A few mothers had "accidentally" thrown them away. When contacted, their sons were able to honestly say they'd never received such a letter. It only delayed their inevitable deployment, but it was better than nothing.

"Mama, do you see it? I'm going to college!" RJ's voice finally seeped through her thoughts. She looked at him still plotting how she could protect him and unsure of what he'd said. Coming out of her trance, she slowly looked down at the envelop that had Tennessee A & I College printed across the top.

"Ma, I'm going to college!" RJ said again, picking her up and spinning her around.

Cora folded and unfolded RJ's clothes, taking inventory, certain he was forgetting something. She tried in vain for weeks to get him to change his mind about abandoning the comforts of home and living on campus.

"What if you get hungry? What if you get sick?" she asked anxiously.

"Ma, I'll be fine. I'm literally twenty minutes away," he said, trying not to laugh.

"Alright, let's get moving boy. I don't want to be in all that campus traffic," Robert Earl rushed, grabbing a box to take down to the truck.

Cora gave him one last inspection. Suitcase.

Backpack. Pillows. And then she started to cry.

"Why is Mama crying?" Memphis asked as she came into his room, hoping to pester him one last time.

"She's happy," RJ said, smiling and putting his arms around Cora.

"Yes, that's right. I'm happy," Cora said, sniffling through a combination of laughter and tears.

"Jeez, I hope she's not this happy when I go to college," Memphis said.

RJ grabbed her and pulled her into the hug, the three of them all laughing.

"Every time I see you, your head is buried in a book," Donna said, taking an uninvited seat next to RJ in the library. A tall, thin, wiry girl with springy blond hair, she'd walked by his table three times trying to get his attention. They had a black history class together and she thought he was cute. She positioned herself closer to him in class, dropped pencils, even feigned a coughing spell, but she remained invisible to him. Taking a page from her modern feminism class, she finally decided to approach him and ask him out.

"Do you have any fun?" she asked. When he

didn't answer, she yanked his notebook from under his hand. A long pencil mark dragged down the page of notes he was taking. "There's a party tonight. I think you and I should go," she continued with one long nervous breath.

RJ looked up at her, annoyed and unmoved by her playful waiting grin.

"I didn't come to college to go to parties or have fun," he said stoically.

"Well, what's the point of waking up every day, walking around and breathing God's air, if you're not having any fun?"

RJ reached unsuccessfully for his notebook, steadying his eyes on her. There was an unconventional cuteness there. Her delicate features complemented her chiseled cheekbones and large hazel eyes. But he didn't need the distraction. He was the first in his family to graduate from high school and now he was the first to go to college. He'd also be the first to have any choices about his future.

"Are you in the habit of asking brothers out?" he asked, like a father chastising his wayward child.

"No," she said defensively. "Only the brothers who aren't smart enough to see a super fine, sophisticated, intelligent Lil Sis right in his face."

RJ took a long pause and looked her up and down.

"And where is this super fine Lil Sis I keep missing?"

She grunted, slung the notebook across the table at him, and bolted up from the chair.

"I'm just playing," he said quickly, realizing the subtle look of hurt on her face. "So, what's your name, super fine sophisticated Lil Sis?" He offered her a smile.

It did sound silly and shallow when he repeated the line her roommate told her to use.

"Donna," she said feeling a sudden rush of embarrassment.

"Nice to meet you Donna; I'm RJ. So, let's talk

about that party tonight."

The drive to Rhode Island was scenic but long. RJ craned his neck and lovingly watched Donna stretch her arms above her head waking from a nap. He was thankful they were almost at her parents' house. After six months of dating, she was eager for him to meet them, especially now.

Although it was Spring, the skies were cloudy and overcast. He felt a chill as they walked hand-in-hand toward the house. The front door opened wide before they even rang the bell. Donna's mother popped out of the house and almost knocked RJ over as she wrapped her arms around Donna.

"Oh, I'm so glad you made it home safely! I can't believe you made that ghastly drive," she said, intentionally looking past RJ. She and her husband offered to buy Donna a plane ticket home for Spring break, but she declined, knowing RJ couldn't afford the flight. He'd done well to scrape up the money for the weekend car rental. She gave Donna a quick inspection, refusing to comment on her outfit that looked like something from one of those urban African street festivals she was starting to hear about. She'd put on a few pounds too. Her mother was sure that was from all that rich Southern fried food she was forced to eat. She was still wracking her brain trying to understand why Donna picked a college all the way in Tennessee.

"I want to be at the epicenter of our heritage," she told her mother.

"I can assure you that none of our heritage is anywhere down there," her mother responded in that way she had of distinguishing their heritage from any that she determined was inferior.

Donna's father squeezed past his wife and gave Donna a hug.

"I see you've put on a little college weight," he said. "Well, let's go inside." He put his arms around Donna's shoulders, leaving RJ trailing behind them.

Her mother ushered them into the sitting room. A short black man in a suit poured them all a glass of tea before retreating to another room. RJ took a nervous sip. It tasted like ice water that had been poured into a glass with leftover day-old tea. He smiled to himself, remembering his mother's comment that Northerners didn't know how to make good sweet iced tea.

"So, you're Robert," her mother started, finally acknowledging his presence.

"Yes ma'am. I actually go by RJ."

"Well, Robert . . . welcome to . . . our home," she said, emphasizing each syllable of his name and pausing between every other word. Her accent, like Donna's, was unlike anything he'd heard before. It sounded elegant but didn't speak to anywhere in particular. At home, he could tell by the accents which part of Tennessee or even Nashville a person was from.

"We're Mr. and Mrs. Washington," she added, both of them finally extending their hands for RJ to shake. She nodded to her husband and, on cue, he began detailing their family's history from England to Rhode Island.

"My ancestors fought in the Revolutionary War," he said with an air of pride that RJ found odd. "For their loyalty, they were given their freedom and the very land this house sits on."

The fact that his family had to be granted freedom by another human being seemed lost on him, but RJ could tell he wouldn't be interested in having a dialogue about the issue. Instead he went on about the church his great-great-grandfather founded, his mother being a school teacher, his father's successful grocery business, and every self-made this or that in between.

"And your people?" he finally asked RJ with a self-satisfied smugness.

"Excuse me?" RJ asked, masking his annoyance at the absurdity of the question.

"From where do they hail?"

"Oh, Tennessee mainly. My mama says we're

rumored to have some ancestry in Cherokee country, but then what black folks don't have some Indian in us," he teased trying to lighten the mood, but no one laughed.

"And what do your parents do?" he pressed, as if he didn't know the answer. He and his wife had already dismissed RJ as soon as they discovered Robert Earl and Cora weren't professionals or even high school graduates. They only agreed to host him for a few days of spring break at Donna's insistence hopeful he was just another of the many college crushes she'd had who would soon disappear. Troubled by the length of her affections toward him and that he was the first boy she'd invited home, her mother had begun to pray for God to speed up his exit.

"I smell something wonderful coming from the kitchen," Donna chimed in hoping to stop the interrogation. "It has to be time for lunch." She took RJ's hand and squeezed it to assure him he was doing fine.

In the dining room, the Washingtons took their seats at each end of the table. It could easily seat ten people and chairs had obviously been removed. RJ and Donna were positioned across from each other. China plates rested on a delicate lace tablecloth, an unnecessary formality, RJ thought. The same man who poured the tea, silently filled water goblets. A woman RJ had not noticed previously followed him with a platter of mixed vegetables. She quickly disappeared only to return moments later carrying another platter with a beautifully browned turkey—the kind you usually only see at Thanksgiving. The butler carved it, and the maid placed a few thin slices on each plate. She made no eye contact until RJ thanked her. Noticeably surprised, she gave him an appreciative nod before disappearing again.

"Dear Lord, we thank you for this bountiful food. Amen," Donna's father prayed.

As they ate in polite silence, RJ scanned the room, wondering how many dreary meals the three of them had actually eaten there. Not wanting to appear to be gawking, he let his eyes dart quickly throughout the room, until he noticed a wood sculptured angel with her arms folded in prayer. The sculpture was no more than two feet tall with deep draping folds at the base that gave it a floating appearance. The expansive wings were intricately carved and arched above the figure's head like a powerful eagle preparing for take-off.

"My Mama would love that," RJ said, rising from the table to get a closer look. The angel was perched on a large family Bible.

"It's been in our family for over seventy years," Donna's mother said, keenly watching RJ's curiosity.

He ran his hand along the ripples of the wings until he noticed Donna delicately clearing her throat as a warning not to touch it.

"I could see her started her morning prayers right here in this corner."

"Your mother is a religious woman?" Donna's

mother asked, with a hint of genuine interest.

"Yes ma'am. Very much so," RJ said. "Prayers first thing in the morning and prayers before she goes to sleep at night. She's a dedicated Baptist."

Donna took a long gulp of water. His religious affiliation was the one thing she'd forgotten to share with her parents.

"Oh, you're Baptist," she said, instantly deflated. "We're Presbyterians."

"My great-great-grandfather's church was the first black Presbyterian church in this community. He had the help of our good white benefactors of course," her father added, preparing a repeat of the family's grand history and all the wonderful white people who helped them along the way.

"We're all Christians of course. Presbyterians, Methodists, Baptists . . . it's just that we've always found the Baptists to be somewhat primitive in their worship," her mother said without pause.

Donna spit up her water and started to cough

uncontrollably.

"Well, they're not pretentious, if that's what you mean," RJ forcefully retorted. He slunk down in his chair. Donna's face was completely flushed as she tried to breathe normally. They suffered through the rest of the meal in silence and left after the weekend with Donna and RJ not sharing their news.

Cora and Robert Earl stood on the porch eagerly waiting for RJ. The sputter of his muffler announced his pending arrival from two houses down. Robert Earl told him every time he came home to let him fix it. Even though he was in college in Nashville, they didn't see him frequently. His studies or community activities always took priority. Cora insisted he at least go to church the first Sunday of the month, and he obeyed, usually. But he opted for a service within walking distance to campus rather than worshiping with the family at their home church. And now there was a girl.

"I think he's really smitten with this girl," Cora said, trying to get a peek at her in the car.

RJ waved at Cora and Robert and scurried around to the passenger side tugging at the sticking door. When he finally got it opened, Donna stepped out wearing a long yellow, purple, and red dress that draped her body like a long sarong. A cluster of gold bracelets dangled from her wrist.

"She look colored to you?" Robert Earl asked with concern in his voice as Donna and RJ walked toward the house holding hands and grinning at each other. "I don't think that girl's colored. And what's she got on?"

"Shush!" Cora said through a frozen smile, not wanting to admit she was wondering the same.

When they reached the gate, RJ loosened Donna's grip on his hand and gave Cora a hug. She lovingly squeezed his face between her hands.

"Look at our college boy," she said proudly.

RJ leaned in to hug Robert Earl, who had not

taken his eyes off Donna as she stood behind RJ, admiring his love for his parents.

"Mama, Daddy, this is Donna," he exhaled her name as though introducing some rare mystical creature.

"It's a pleasure to meet you both," she said. She extended her hand unsure as to whether a hug was welcome or expected.

The four of them stood on the porch for a few seconds inspecting each other.

"Are you colored?" Robert Earl finally abrasively asked.

"Pop!" RJ started to rebuke him. But Donna touched his arm and gently laughed.

"Yes sir. I am Black. Just a little lighter package than most."

"Not that it matters," Cora chimed in.

"Like hell it don't," Robert huffed. Cora slapped his arm.

"Not that it matters at all," she repeated. "Now

come on in this house. I've got some homemade banana pudding on the table."

Placing herself between RJ and Donna, Cora looped arms with them.

"Have you ever had real Southern banana pudding?" she asked Donna as they walked into the house. She gave Robert Earl a cross look, admonishing him not to say one more word.

"No ma'am," Donna said, still amused.

"Well you're in for a treat. Tell her RJ."

"My mama makes the best banana pudding this side of the Cumberland River," he said, giving her a kiss on the cheek.

RJ and Donna got married in a simple affair at the campus chapel surrounded by a handful of close friends, Cora, and Robert Earl. Memphis stood beside Donna as her junior maid of honor. Memphis didn't know what that was, but she was thrilled when Donna offered her what sounded like an esteemed and grownup position. From the altar, as they stood together before taking their vows, Donna watched the door, hoping her parents would come. Cora was taken by how much RJ looked like a young, handsome Robert Earl in his black suit with a white rose in the lapel that matched Donna's free flowing white dress. The dress would have swallowed Donna under normal circumstances. But the night they came to the house and RJ swore he'd found his soulmate and couldn't wait—not even for the one year he had left in college— to make her his wife, Cora knew love wasn't the only thing driving them to the altar so quickly.

They exited the chapel under a shower of rice and well wishes.

"Lord keep a covering over them," Cora prayed silently as they drove off in their decorated rental car.

RJ and Donna, dressed in matching dashikis, laid out their case before a table covered in imitation African artifacts.

"Imagine the chance to smell the air, touch the soil, and meet the people where things like these came from," RJ said.

Robert Earl sucked a piece of orange through his teeth, scrunching his face at the unexpected sourness.

"Your Mama and me spent over $100 on them encyclopedias. Anything you wanna know about Africa ought to be in them books," he scoffed.

"We'll get to meet our people. Learn about our roots."

"Pssh," he scoffed, a squirt of juice running down his chin. "Your roots are right here in Tennessee. Besides, I thought naming this boy Sad-ee-kay" he slowed down each syllable of the name he refused to call his grandson and still got it wrong, "was your way of getting in touch with your roots."

"It's Sadiqq Pop, Suh-deek." He turned to his mother, not wanting to restart a debate that began at Sadiqq's birth. "Mama, a whole group of professors are going. It's just four weeks. If nothing else, think of what it will do for my career."

"I think they should go," Memphis piped up. She flung a set of red, black, and green beads she'd grabbed from the table around her neck. "And bring me something back."

"Well, nobody asked you, now did they," Robert Earl spat out more harshly than expected.

Sadiqq lay on the floor, oblivious to the fact that he was the topic of all the conversation. The heels of his feet toward the ceiling, he made roaring noises as he rolled his toy truck back and forth across the carpet. Cora couldn't bring herself to admit it out loud, but she agreed with Robert Earl. Nothing could be out there so incredible that it was worth leaving your baby behind for a month.

"We wouldn't ask if this weren't so special. It really is once in a lifetime," Donna finally spoke up. She hadn't wanted to ask them or anybody else to watch Sadiqq. She wanted to take him with them. But he was only three years old, and the university wouldn't risk the liability. There also would be no one to watch him while they spent their days beneath the earth's surface, searching for mysterious ancient treasures. "But if it's too much, we understand. We can ask one of the graduate students," she said feigning exhausted defeat, knowing that if her only option was leaving her son with a nameless, clock-watching, list-checker the way her parents had done when they took one of their yearly jaunts to Europe, she wouldn't be going.

Cora shook her head furiously and patted Sadiqq's head. He looked up from his truck and smile as she handed him a piece of butterscotch. His favorite, just like RJ.

"You know we'll watch our favorite grandbaby," she said with a heavy sigh, tickling him under his chin.

"Thanks, Mama. You're the best," RJ hugged her. Donna leaned in and grabbed them both, pulling a reluctant Robert Earl into the huddle. Memphis sprang to her feet and wrapped them all in her long arms. Not one to miss hug time, Sadiqq squeezed in between their legs.

"Me, too," he demanded in that self-confident toddler way. They all laughed.

Chapter 20

My brethren, count it all joy when you fall into various trials, knowing that the testing of your faith produces patience. But let patience have its perfect work that you may be perfect and complete, lacking nothing.

—James 1:2-4

Cora bolted straight up in the bed, gasping for air. The dark room was rotating clockwise as the ceiling started to slowly descend on her head. Keep breathing. Keep breathing. Why wasn't Robert Earl moving? She reached for him, but the whirling was picking up speed and she felt like she was in the spin cycle of a washing machine, grasping for nonexistent walls to steady herself from falling into the floor that was sinking beneath her. Keep breathing. Keep breathing. The phone was ringing. The room was spinning. Keep breathing. Keep breathing.

Robert Earl finally moved. Keep breathing. Keep breathing.

RJ and Donna are dead, the thick accented voice on the other end of the phone said softly.

And then everything stopped.

Cora ran to the bathroom, shaking and holding her stomach. She felt as though she were about to vomit up her insides as she fell to the floor and leaned against the tub.

"How much more can you punish me, Lord?! How much more." She hit her hands against the tub, hoping the cold pain would wake her from a nightmare. "Take me. Take my life, just bring my boy back to me, Lord!"

Memphis rested her head on Cora's shoulder and Sadiqq stretched his body across her lap. Sadiqq fixed his eyes on the long brown box holding his father. Cora told him his daddy was sleeping and on his way to Heaven. He wondered why he was sleeping in a long box and, more important, when he'd wake up.

Cora stared into the pulpit while the pastor offered words of comfort over RJ's body. Donna's parents insisted she be funeralized at their family church and likewise buried with four generations of her ancestors "here in the United States of America." The edge in their grief-stricken voices made it all too clear that they blamed RJ for dragging their daughter across the world to a forsaken desert where an ill-equipped pilot would send them to their death. They would not be at RJ's funeral, nor did they want any part of his family at Donna's. Robert Earl told them to go to hell.

Cora walked stiffly pass Robert Earl, Memphis, and Sadiqq and the church members who had descended on the house to continue offering their condolences. Retreating to her bedroom, she locked the door, peeled off her funeral clothes, and climbed into bed.

"Cora, you need anything?" Lil Sis called softly through the door.

Cora rolled over and pulled the covers over her head without answering. She didn't want to talk, not even to God, afraid to verbalize the rage that burned within her and equally afraid of the voices in her head screaming for her to demand God return RJ and take the sin—Memphis.

"Weeping may endure for a night, but joy comes in the morning," she could still hear the preacher saying.

But sleep offered no comfort as she tossed and turned, watching the moon overtake the sun only to see the sun rise again. she pulled at her hair and banged her head against the bed rails.

"She been in there for three days," Lil Sis said with concern in her voice.

"I know," Robert Earl said hanging his head. "I figure she'll come out when she's ready."

"Cora, it's me Lil Sis. You alright in there?" she asked nervously. She sat by the door, listening helplessly to Cora's low wailing moans that were growing more intense along with jarring successive thumps against the wall.

"Robert Earl, break down the door," she finally said, her voice trembling.

"I ain't tearing down this door and owing money we ain't got," he said defiantly, trying to hide his own fear. Caving to her pleas, he took a screwdriver and jimmied the lock, quickly walking away before Lil Sis could open the door.

Cora sat on the floor in her slip with her legs tucked under her, rocking, pulling at her hair, and banging her head against the wall. Lil Sis knelt beside her and moved her arms around Cora's shoulders as they rocked together.

"Why? Why did God have to take RJ!" Cora screamed, letting her head fall into Lil Sis's chest.

A flock of jubilant souls piled into the church for the final night of revival. Even the biggest sinners couldn't escape the deep, pulsating sound of the church organ vibrating through the neighborhood and shaming those who refused to join worship service to at least take their card games and beer indoors.

Cora gripped her Bible so tightly that her fingertips started to cramp, giving her some relief from the dull numbness of grief that was choking her. The preacher, a tall scarecrow of a man vising from Georgia, perched himself in the pulpit, beckoning the Holy Spirit.

The choir began to sway in sync as a voice from the row of black-suited deacons called out, "Father . . . I . . . stretch . . . my hands to thee."

The choir responded, "No other help I know." And continued singing, substituting most of the words for low, gut-wrenching groans.

Tears began trickling down Cora's cheeks. She didn't feel herself moving from the wooden pews to the altar, but the warmth of the hovering church mothers and deacons rushed through her body like a jolt of lightening as the preacher cupped the top of her head with the palm of his hand and smeared a woody smelling oil across her forehead. It ran down her brow and mixed with the tears, forming a salty paste.

"Let it out, Lil Sis! Let the Holy Spirit have His way," the preacher commanded.

Cora trembled and fell to her knees. She tried to speak, but it felt like a lake of burning lava was running down her throat.

"Release it!" he shouted again. "Give it to God!"

Cora gasped for air, dropping her head to her knees, feeling the preacher's grip growing tighter. The encircled crowd began stuttering unrecognizable words and sounds.

"Help me, Jesus," she squeezed out, before collapsing to the floor.

Cora sat alone at the kitchen table. The house was

asleep, quite without the usual busyness of Sunday mornings of Cora rushing through the house with flour-covered hands, calling everyone to the breakfast table before Sunday school. A memory of RJ whining at the table, pulling at his tie and insisting on strawberry jelly, raced through Cora's mind. RJ only ate strawberry jelly.

She rose from the table and frantically searched the refrigerator. She pulled out foil-covered plates and casserole dishes and reached past a jug of milk to find a jar of strawberry jelly pressed toward the back. She admired it in her hands. And then, carefully, as if the contents were fragile, she opened the lid. A small well had been scooped out of the top where RJ had hastily put some on a piece of toast before he and Donna dashed to the airport.

"It's a long flight. You need more to eat," she called after him from the front door.

"No time mama. Love you," he said before ducking into the car.

She held the jar to her nose, inhaling the syrupy sweet scent before starting to cry. Tears dropped from her face onto the jar and rolled down the side. She finally pressed her head on the table and finished her cry in the crevice of her folded arms. There was no sound, just tears that she offered up to God, hoping that might be enough to finally satisfy Him. Was she not entitled to some mercy? Feeling a hand pulling at her elbow, she opened her eyes to find Sadiqq standing in front of her in his cartoon covered pajamas. She sat up and unfolded her arms as he climbed into her lap. Holding her face inside his little palms, he mashed his face against hers, his big, dark eyes staring into her and reminding her of RJ.

"Grandma no cry," he said before climbing down with the tireless energy of a toddler and looking around the kitchen as if he were about to dive into an unexpected adventure.

"Sandwich, please," he said, pointing to the jar of jelly on the table.

Chapter 21

Memphis stood inspecting herself in the mirror, fussing over the tassel on her cap that kept swooping into her eyes. Her tall, lean frame had shaped into a young woman.

"I want to go to college with you," Sadiqq charged into her room. He jumped on her bed, snatched the cap off her head and plopped it on his own.

"Make those good grades and you will," she said, clasping the bottom of his chin in her hand and squeezing it adoringly.

"Boy, quit bothering your Auntie Memphis.

She's got to get ready now," Cora came in from the hallway, carrying a small black box with a red ribbon. She handed it to Memphis. Inside was a pair of small white pearl earrings. Memphis knew they probably weren't real, but they were real enough for her.

"I'm going to miss you, Mama," she said, throwing her hands around her neck.

"Well there are some perfectly good schools around her," Cora reminded her.

Memphis gave her a sideways grin, exposing the dimple in her cheek.

"Mama, I'm going to Howard."

Cora mustered a light laugh, determined not to cry. She didn't mention to Memphis that she used to work on the campus. It was so long ago, more than thirty years. And what would she care about her mother having been a cook? She was going to get a degree, from the school she set her sights on after coming home from a school trip raving about the city, the campus, and the people. Robert Earl griped about the costs until she won a scholarship thanks to Miss Lillian who somehow had come to serve on the university's board.

*****

Madison scoffed at all the pink and white ruffled pillows her mother arranged on each twin bed, giving no thought to what her roommate might want. The room looked like an explosion of cotton candy.

"What if she doesn't like pink?" Madison offered.

"Please, what girl doesn't like pink," her mother responded, continuing to make the bed. She threw down a shaggy white rug and began pulling neatly-pressed pink floral curtains from a plastic hanging bag.

"*Mom . . .*," her already high-pitched voice rising.

"You know your mother and I are just so proud to have you here at our alma mater," Thurston said, hoping to ward off another mother and daughter debate like he'd suffered through on the trip from New York.

"I know, Daddy," she said exasperated.

"Besides, when we leave, you can take it all down," he said, giving her a sly wink.

"Oh, don't encourage her," Harriet scolded, glaring at him.

Students were milling about excitedly searching for room numbers and hauling suitcases and crates. Harriet had them all so engaged in helping to hang the curtains that they didn't hear Madison walk in to the room that looked like an explosion of cotton candy. She dropped her two suitcases on the floor and scanned the room unsure of which bed was hers. The thump of her suitcases hitting the floor made them all turn her way.

Madison abandoned her side of the curtain rod, causing the whole thing to collapse and jumped to attention to greet Memphis.

"Hi, I'm Madison," she said, leaning in for an unexpected hug. "You can change everything when she leaves," she whispered in Memphis's ear.

"Memphis," she said, nodding in amusement as she pulled away and offered a handshake. They stood almost eye to eye and admired each other's unruly sandy brown hair. They shared an odd familiarity.

Harriet had come down from the step ladder, giving up on getting the curtains up alone, and began trying to tame Madison's hair as if she were meeting a blind date instead of a dorm mate. Madison brushed her hand away with a big show of annoyance.

"Memphis did you say?" her mother asked.

"Yes, ma'am."

"Well, excuse our mess. We've been setting up all morning."

She waited for Memphis to comment on the room. When she didn't, Harriet proudly said, "I hope you don't mind. I thought it would be nice if the room matched."

"Yes, ma'am. It's very nice. Thank you."

She displayed a satisfied grin, nodding to Madison who rolled her eyes for Memphis' benefit.

"Can we help you and your family bring some of your things up?" Thurston politely asked.

"No sir, thank you. This is it," she said, pointing to the two suitcases still sitting in the middle of the floor.

Harriet looked expectantly at the door. "Well, where are your parents? We have to meet them before we leave."

"They weren't able to make the trip," Memphis said, trying to cover the hint of disappointment.

Harriet looked quizzically at Memphis's generic sneakers and worn blue jeans, making her feel as though she were being inspected for quality control. She could tell them she dressed comfortably for the 30-hour bus ride from Tennessee, but she wasn't sure what purpose that would serve.

"Well . . . I don't believe we've properly introduced ourselves," her mother said, clearing her throat and sounding more formal. "We're *Doctor* and Mrs. Edwards," she said, overemphasizing her husband's profession.

"And they were just leaving," Madison chimed in before her mother could begin the inquisition scene that was developing in her imagination.

Madison and Memphis cleaned up the last remnants of an impromptu pizza party. The pulsing heaviness of synthesized beats over scatting lyricists had drawn most of the wing to their room. As they poured in, most discovered they already knew each other from summer vacations on Martha's Vineyard or Jack and Jill cotillions. Memphis had disappeared amidst their hyper chatter and she was thankful when they all finally retreated to their rooms.

"My mother hates hip hop music," Madison said, turning off the portable stereo. She had already stripped the beds and covered her side of the room with posters of half-naked men, making Memphis blush.

"Cigarette?" she offered Memphis.

"No thanks, I don't smoke."

"Eh, me neither, unless the occasion calls for it. She put the pack of cigarettes back in her purse, fell on her bed, and thumbed through her collection of cassette tapes.

"So what kind of name is Memphis?" she asked cutting right to things.

"I could ask you the same about Madison," Memphis said, unsure as to whether she should be insulted.

"It's my mother's maiden name. Her way of holding on to it. She should have hyphenated, but I guess women didn't do that back then."

She felt a little bad about clearly jumping to the wrong conclusion too quickly.

"My mother said I was conceived the night my father surprised her and came home early from Memphis."

"Oh, well that's kind of romantic. But then thinking about your parents being romantic . . ."

"Eww," they said simultaneously and erupted into full laughter.

"Why did you come all the way to Howard from Tennessee?" Madison probed more, passing Memphis some cookies her mother had baked and rubbing away the tears left from her laughter.

"Same as you, I guess. It's a great school, full of opportunities and so much history of our people."

Madison raised her brow. Howard hadn't been a choice for her. It was an expectation. For her brother too, only he had been bold enough to rebel and choose Morehouse.

"Well, my father will love you," she said when Memphis told her of her plan to go to medical school after graduation. "As for me, I'm going into politics. Maybe I'll help get the first black or woman elected president. They both laughed even harder.

"What kind of parents don't come see their daughter off to college?" Harriet pondered, setting aside the book she was only pretending to read.

"The kind who work for a living," Thurston said over his newspaper. He always waited until the end of the day to read the morning's news, and pages were scattered about the bed as he discarded each finished section.

"Well, *we* work dear," she shot back.

He gave his wife an amused glance. She hadn't worked since the children were born. She'd dabbled with his account books, usually upset that he'd allowed someone to take so long to pay off a medical bill, and helped keep his small office neat and tidy when he first opened his practice. Now he had a staff, a full clinic, and unlimited privileges at the hospital. The most she'd done this year was smile alongside him while they cut a ribbon to the entrance of their new building with a pair of oversized, nonfunctioning scissors.

"Oh, you know what I mean," she said, sensing his unspoken sarcasm and slapping him on the arm. "I wonder . . .," she stopped as though paralyzed by a particularly frightening thought. "What if she is one of those first-generation students the university has committed to helping this year?"

Thurston had served on the special committee of the Trustee Board formed after members of the community publicly questioned whether the university was doing enough for the next generation.

"Is our only focus descendants of the talented 10th or helping to develop another great generation of talented 10th?" the president had as asked emphatically as a vote was put before the body about reserving fifteen admission spots for first-generation students from underprivileged backgrounds. Generation Next they'd called the pilot project.

"She could be. If so, mission accomplished," amused by his wife's over analysis.

Harriet rubbed her chin with her forefinger, deep in thought. "This girl could be from anywhere. You saw what she had on. We don't know anything about her or her people," she said, growing more worried.

She commended Thurston for voting in favor of the initiative when he told her about it, but she hadn't imagined that *those* students would comingle with the rest. He was particularly naïve about these things, she thought. She watched the news and read stories in her *Ebony* magazine about the drugs, violence, and teenage pregnancies that plagued America's black ghettos. She'd even heard a story about one young black boy getting admitted to one of the country's top universities only to lose his basketball scholarship in a matter of months after it was discovered he was running a drug operation from his dorm room. The university didn't know he was a gang member.

"Dear God, think of the influence she could have on Madison." Her thoughts running wild.

Thurston was growing annoyed.

"Perhaps she'll be a better influence than some of the girls Madison has grown up with." He had upheld medical confidentiality and not shared with

Harriet the number of discreet courtesy calls he'd made for the daughters of golfing friends, church members, and Harriet's social club partners. He kept secret the marijuana he caught Madison hiding in her purse the night of her cotillion. She swore the girls had only planned to try it that one night after the dance with their dates and begged him not to tell her mother as she shamefully handed over the small packet to him. Maybe Harriet had forgotten about their own son being arrested for underage drinking and the horror of going to the New York Police Department in the middle of the night. A captain who recognized him from his son's elite high school swim team nudged Thurston in the ribs. "Boys will be boys right," before releasing him with only a warning.

He rolled over and turned off the light. He was done talking about nothing.

Chapter 22

Robert Earl's feet were tired from walking all over the campus trying to find one shady spot to watch the graduation ceremony. Now that it was over, he was in no mood to weave through crowds of parents, pausing every minute so as not to interrupt their photographs, and look for Memphis.

"That girl knows we're here," he said irritably as he trailed behind Cora and Sadiqq who were paying him no attention.

"I see her," Sadiqq called out, racing toward a large group of people in the middle of the courtyard.

When Cora and Sadiqq reached her, Memphis wrapped her arms around them both and searched for her father who was moving slowly in the distance. It had been two years since they'd seen her, although she called every Sunday when the long distance rates were cheaper. Cora studied the large, untamed curly afro that framed her chiseled face, wondering how she managed to keep her graduation cap in place. Gold hoop earrings peeked from underneath her hair. Cora didn't know she'd gotten her ears pierced.

Memphis excitedly pulled Cora and Sadiqq into the middle of the crowd.

"Mama, this is Madison, my roommate," she said smiling and interlocking her arms with hers. She had the same bushy afro and a colorful drape across her graduation gown.

"I've heard so much about you," Madison said, offering her a hug.

Curious, Cora thought. Memphis had told them very little about Madison or her family other than the father was a doctor and the mother was an uptight bourgeois socialite who had finally warmed to her after she joined them for Thanksgiving and demonstrated proper manners. She knew the girls had grown, close and she wondered what exactly Memphis had told her about them. The truth was, not much. When asked what her parents did for a living, Memphis always simply said her mother was in the service industry and her father a vehicle technician. It wasn't that she was ashamed of them. She had just watched the look her classmates had given students like her who admitted their parents were housekeepers, cooks, or warehouse workers. That look of how sad for you, maybe you'll still amount to something one day, before walking away and dismissing their relevance. She'd caught the same expression among some of the professors.

"Let me introduce you to my parents. They've been dying to meet you," Madison said, disappearing into the crowd of people. By then Robert Earl had caught up. He gave Memphis a stiff hug and said,

"Congratulations," just as Madison emerged locked arm-in-arm with her father after unsuccessfully trying to pull her mother from a conversation with a young lawyer and his family whom she had planned for Madison to get to know quite well over the summer.

"Daddy, these are Memphis's parents," she announced.

Cora and Thurston stood frozen, facing each other. Her mouth slightly agape, she couldn't release any sound, but extended her hand to him in slow motion. He held it, staying transfixed on her face until Robert Earl let out a raspy cough.

"I'm Robert Earl, her husband," he said prompting Thurston to release Cora's hand in exchange for Robert Earl's.

"Yes . . . nice . . . to meet you," he said, gathering his composure. He looked over his shoulder and found Harriet still trying to entice the young man with Madison's accolades. "This is Harriet," he said as he guided her away from the one-sided conversation. "My

260

wife."

"Oh yes, Memphis's family. Delighted," she said placing her hand over her chest as if meeting them had just warmed her heart. "You must be very proud of your daughter." Even while talking to them, her eyes dotted around the courtyard, hoping the lawyer and his family wouldn't get too far out of sight, but it was too late. They had already disappeared into the masses.

"So, is Memphis your only child?" Harriet asked, resolved to resume her bidding in the evening at the president's reception for distinguished alumni and donors.

Cora and Robert Earl were never sure how to answer that question, not that they went many places where they were asked.

"Yes," Robert Earl said sharply.

Thurston remembered Cora speaking about a son and a daughter that night—that night he hadn't forgotten. Cora could feel his questioning eyes.

"We had two other children," Cora said, pushing

down a lump in her throat and finding her voice again. "They passed away."

For the first time, Harriet actually looked at her and shared a graceful moment of understanding, remembering her miscarried child.

"I'm very sorry," she said, her tone softer and focused.

"Thank you," Cora managed a smile and a quick, almost unnoticeable, glance to Thurston who had only taken his eyes off her long enough to avoid Robert Earl's uncomfortable glare.

"And this is our grandson," Cora quickly added, determined not to let the day of celebration sink in sadness. Sadiqq jumped around Memphis, knocking her cap off her afro. He was ten now and almost to her chest. She ducked and dodged his playful hands before finally handing him the cap.

"Well, he's just adorable," Harriet said. When he scrunched up his face, she offered an apology. "I mean handsome, of course." Sadiqq gave her a grin, exposing the missing side tooth that was just starting to grow back in.

Robert Earl had gone back to complaining. Now he was ready to eat.

"And I want some real food," he barked. "You'd think with all this tuition this school charges they would have something more than cookies and punch."

"Robert Earl!" Cora said under her breath, lowering her head in embarrassment.

Harriet was amused by his simplicity and had already sized them both up as country bumpkins, the cute kind, usually unaware that they were being used for entertainment.

"Well, we have to rush off as well. We have to get back to the hotel and get ready for tonight's president's reception," she said turning to Thurston and Madison. "It's invitation only."

Robert Earl started to grumble something under his breath and Cora delicately nudged him. Before either of her parents could say another word, Madison thrust her camera at her father and ordered him to take photos of her and Memphis. It was then, looking at the girls from behind the camera lens that he saw it for the first time, the striking resemblance. Same hair. Same eyes. Same dimpled smile. He moved the camera from his face and, adjusting his eyes, turned to Cora. Could it be?

Cora walked among the buildings, passing early morning workers furiously tearing down the stage, stacking chairs, and returning the campus back to normal. Nothing was as Cora remembered. But then it had been almost thirty years since she'd stepped onto the yards of the campus. At seventeen years old, she was expecting something great to happen. Now she couldn't even remember what it had felt like to be seventeen, not even as she stood by the tall oak tree she'd spent the morning trying to find. She circled around it, running her hands against the tough bark.

Some students had carved their initials into it, marking their love affair.

"Perhaps we should have put our initials on it," a voice said from behind her. She was both surprised and not so surprised to find Thurston standing there.

"What are you doing here?" she asked.

"Hoping to find you."

They stood awkwardly together, hesitantly hugging and unsure of what they were afraid of.

"Cora . . .," Thurston started, searching her eyes.

"Imagine, our daughters roommates here at Howard. Who would have thought?" she interrupted matter-of-factly, trying to avoid any belated sentimentalism.

"Cora, is Memphis . . ."

"Robert Earl is Memphis's daddy," she said decisively and not letting him speak the question she knew he wanted to ask.

"But I . . ."

"Robert Earl is her daddy and there's nothing more to say about that."

Cora had made up her mind that Memphis was as much Robert Earl's as Roberta had been hers, and there was no one to say otherwise. Putting the question out there would change nothing.

"Cora, I'm sorry for everything," Thurston said. He had been a coward. Afraid to tell his parents he was in love with an uneducated university cook. Afraid to turn around and pack Cora into his car that night he watched her slink into the pitiful run down house in Black Bottom. Afraid to look back and to hurt Harriet. Cora was right. Robert Earl was Memphis's father.

He looked at his watch. Harriet would be up soon. They were having brunch with the lawyer and his family. He didn't know where Cora was staying. He imagined in one of those cheaper places on the outskirts of the city.

"Can I give you a ride somewhere?" he asked.

"I think I'm going to sit here for a while," she

said. She had an hour before the next bus and welcomed being alone with her thoughts before returning to the hotel to hear Robert Earl's snoring and Sadiqq clamoring for the TV to watch cartoons.

Thurston paused and held his hand against the side of her face. She closed her eyes and placed her hand over his, taking in the warmth before pulling away.

"Goodbye, Thurston." She turned her back, choosing not to watch him walk away.

*****

Miss Lillian and Mr. Jameson had argued all morning. It was the same argument they'd been having all week about her 50th birthday party. She wanted Cora there as her guest for the evening affair, not as a servant.

"Absolutely not," he bellowed. There was enough murmuring about Lillian's extreme embrace of Cora's family after Roberta's death. Flowers were an expected show of decency and even paying the funeral costs was a kind gesture for such loyal help. But to drive into Black Bottom carrying food and sit front row at the church with the family, was evidence that her evolution into a proper southern wife was still a work in progress. And with the agitation of Dr. King and the civil rights movement making the city's blacks more emboldened, his boss made clear that she needed to get Lillian in line if he wanted to make vice president.

"Cora is not just my cook and housekeeper. She's a friend," Lillian shot back.

"No. She *is* just your cook and housekeeper," he corrected, holding up his hand to silence any further discussion as if she were a child.

Lillian was so mad that she took her kitchen shears and cut off the tops of the pre-birthday roses he had bought her, leaving only a dozen lone stems in the vase.

"No Cora, no party," she said defiantly.

"Fine Lillian, just fine. I'll cancel your party," he said as he stormed out of the house.

It seemed like only a few minutes had passed

when his office called. His secretary found him on the floor. Lillian needed to hurry to the hospital, but it was already too late when she arrived. Like a stray leaf caught by a sudden and unexpected wind, her husband was gone. A massive heart attack, the doctor told her.

She sat on her veranda watching the birds dance between the trees that framed the backyard.

The house was empty. Lonely. Sad.

A son would be nice right about now, she thought, reminded of the babies she lost and her refusal to give up the one thing she could control and try "just once more" when he'd pleaded.

A bumble bee whizzed by her head, distracting her thoughts. She swatted at it, forcing it to circle around her pitcher of sweet tea. Before it could make a landing, Cora eased behind Miss Lillian and killed it off with a towel she had draped over her shoulder. Cora stood quietly, holding a small German chocolate cake—Miss Lillian's favorite. Miss Lillian stared at her and tried to squeeze out a weak "Thank you" from her throat.

When nothing came out, she threw her arms around Cora and rested her head on her shoulder. Cora let her cry.

Miss Lillian's lawn looked like an overpriced flea market, with sofas, lamps, and dining chairs placed in no particular order. Wearing nothing more than pajamas, she hauled boxes of clothes to the curb. The morning parade of housekeepers eyed her suspiciously as she invited them to take what they wanted. "Is that your white lady?" one whispered to Cora as they got off the bus together.

"Miss Lillian?" Cora started toward her as she furiously pulled blouses and sweaters from one box to another.

"Cora, you're here! Please help me with these things," she said excitedly.

"Why don't we go inside and get you some clothes," Cora said warmly, trying to mask her concern.

Miss Lillian stopped and looked at herself. She smiled shyly at Cora, realizing her appearance.

"Well, I guess the whole neighborhood probably thinks I've lost my mind," she said, allowing Cora to guide her toward the house. She slid into a robe and slippers. The house was stripped of most of the furniture. What remained was draped in large sheets. Two coffee cups sat alone on the kitchen counter. She poured coffee into both, passing a warm cup to Cora.

"You believe in God, don't you Cora?" she asked, sipping from the cup Cora recognized as Mr. Jameson's.

"Yes, ma'am," she said.

Miss Lillian hadn't considered herself an atheist or a Christian. The truth is, she had never really given God much thought, although she always stopped to listen whenever Cora started an impromptu song to Jesus. She had a nice voice and the words always seemed to delight her while she rolled out biscuits in the kitchen. A few times, especially after Roberta's death, Lillian caught a glimpse of her crying through a prayer.

"Have you ever wondered why you were born? What you were put you here on this Earth to do?"

Cora had wondered that most of her life, and she still wasn't sure of the answer. Some days she felt as though she was here just to suffer one indignity after another.

"I supposed only God knows, ma'am," she said.

"Exactly!" Miss Lilian said, her eyes dancing wildly. "And I talked to your God last night. Know what He told me?"

Cora shook her head.

"That I've been asleep for twenty-five years and it's time to wake up!" She took an excited breath, pausing to give Cora time to say something. When she didn't, she let out a heavy sigh.

"You think I've gone mad?"

"No, ma'am," Cora said earnestly. She had heard the voice. The still, calm, inaudible voice that couldn't be explained, only experienced. "What does God want you to do?"

Miss Lillian perked up again. "I'm closing up the house and going to Europe to find my purpose," she announced as though she were planning a landing to Mars. I'm donating everything I can. Be a dear and help me pack up these dishes?" she asked politely.

"Yes, ma'am."

"And please . . . don't . . . call me ma'am anymore," she insisted.

There were only about ten years between them, with Cora being the younger of the two, even though she felt much older with stands of gray hair already peeking in around the roots. Of course, Miss Lillian would have had a few gray hairs as well if not for her weekly trips to the beauty parlor.

She handed Cora a box and started moving frantically through the kitchen.

"I leave tomorrow," she said almost as an afterthought.

"Tomorrow!" Cora repeated in an unexpected panic that reminded Miss Lillian of what she'd put in the kitchen drawer.

"Don't worry about working while I'm gone," she said, handing her an envelope. "This should get you through the next six months. And if you need more, I'll have my bank wire some to you."

Cora's heart settled. "Thank you, ma . . .," Miss Lillian gave her a scolding, corrective look. "Thank you, Miss Lillian."

Cora sat at the kitchen table, fanning the bills of money through her fingers. She had never held $3,000 and was counting it for a fourth time. There was enough to cover Sadiqq's tuition and send a little to Memphis, not that she needed it; but she was working so hard at the hospital. She could finally pay off the furniture bill—nothing more than two lamps, a chair, and a sofa, but they would be hers. And the house, Mr. Ray told her and Robert Earl that after all these years of renting, he'd sell them the house for just $900. The rest of the money was going in the bank. Yes, tomorrow while Miss Lillian sailed off on her European adventure, Cora was going to open up her first bank account.

Robert Earl sucked air between his teeth and roughly slid his chair back from the kitchen table.

"What are you supposed to do for two months?" he asked as he wiped the morning breakfast from his mouth.

Cora had never had a vacation. She could barely remember a time when she wasn't working or doing something for somebody. She hadn't had the luxury of sleeping through life, but it was definitely passing her by.

"Anything I feel like," she told him matter-of-factly.

She took her newspaper and cup of coffee, sat on the porch, and watched a line of her neighbors head to the bus stop. They all exchanged pleasant good mornings. All the maids had heard the ladies they cleaned and cooked for whispering about Miss Lillian and her "breakdown." They also heard about the "insane amount of money she gave her Negroes."

"Cora, child, you got it made. Enjoy yourself!" one neighbor yelled back at her.

With the morning settled down and Robert Earl out of the house, she went into the bedroom and rummaged through a set of boxes in the back of her closet. She opened the lid to one that had RJ's name scribbled across it. Pleasant memories raced through her mind as she held his diploma and school awards. She drew his cap and gown to her and exhaled. It still smelled like him. In the bottom of the box was her book, *The Souls of Black Folks*. She remembered his little hands clutching it, pretending to read while she rocked and fed Memphis. Tears fell down her face as she rustled through the stiff pages and found handwritten notes in the margin where RJ had read it in college. She held the book close to her then stretched out on her bed, not moving until she had finally finished it herself.

The next day, left in the quiet of the house, she returned to her closet, this time finding the tattered box of books Thurston had given her. She sat on her porch, each day, reading until she'd finished them all.

*****

Robert Earl hadn't been to Jake's in a long time. The place hadn't changed much. Same bare folding tables and lawn chairs with missing rings in the seat that swallowed your butt uncomfortably if you didn't sit just right. Fumes from the crackling barbecue pit out back trailed through the screen door and filled the room with sweet smoke. The good liquor was hidden behind a large pool table in the corner, and Robert Earl was sure Jake had never gotten his liquor license. You could join a good card game, although the price had jumped from fifty cents to five dollars over the years. And Jake still had the pretty girls around to light cigarettes, pour drinks, and serve hot pulled pork sandwiches, even though most of the men there were now at an age where they were nothing more than amusing old flirts with open wallets for tips. Robert Earl wasn't quite washed up. He could still attract the ladies. He just no longer had the energy for the chase.

He ordered another drink as the dealer floated a fresh hand across the table. It was getting late, but he'd pocketed $25 so far. Besides, Cora didn't care what time he came home anymore. She hadn't cared in a long time, and that was nobody's fault but his own. They had settled into a comfortable understanding. He stretched and excused himself to the restroom after pocketing another modest win. He stood looking at himself in the large cracked mirror over the sink. Every mistake, regret, and sin was etched in his face and he wondered where a lifetime had gone. Sadiqq was rarely home, spending most of his time at the campus library or leading a protest about something neither Robert Earl nor Cora understood. Memphis was busy with her medical residency and her Sunday calls were growing shorter. Robert Earl missed hearing Sadiqq's heavy feet running up the stairs. To his surprise, he even missed Memphis's high-pitched rambling at the dinner table and the racket of her stereo that he'd threatened to smash into pieces when the blaring music woke him from a nap. This was the sentimental loneliness of pursuing old age he imagined, before collapsing to the floor.

*****

Memphis timidly knocked on the Director's door, her eyes puffy and red. She hadn't expected to cry as much as she did when her mother called.

"Sorry to bother you Dr. Edwards, but I have to go home," she said.

Thurston looked up from this desk and offered her a glass of water, seeing that she was upset.

"What's wrong?" he asked, concerned.

"My father just died," she said solemnly before starting to weep again.

*****

Robert Earl looked as dignified and strong as he had the day he marched through the city square in his Army uniform. His funeral was a reunion of former Black Bottom neighbors and friends, and Cora suspected a few ex-girlfriends too. Even Miss Lillian made it back. Just three months into her trip, she walked into the church arm-in-arm with a short, squatty brown-skinned man. Memphis stood at the casket, beside Cora, greeting guests and politely taking in some of the memories his friends paused briefly to share. She wept a few times, and Cora gently put her arm around her shoulders, reminding her to be strong. Certain that the pastor, who only saw Robert Earl on Easter and Christmas, couldn't know his grandfather as well as he did, Sadiqq insisted on doing the eulogy. The unorthodox move caused a few raised eyebrows in the church, until he had the congregation up on their feet and waving their hands with praise. He'd been reading and studying his Bible. Cora could tell.

"Yes sir" and "Preach boy" was echoed

throughout the pews. When he finished, he used one of Robert Earl's handkerchiefs to rub sweat from his forehead and placed it on the casket before leading the family out of the church.

"It was a beautiful service," Miss Lillian said, helping Cora slice the apple spice cake she'd grabbed from the baker en route from the airport.

"Bellisimo," said the strange man who'd been following Miss Lillian around all day. Cora was able to take a closer look at him now. He had a thin layer of black and silver hair he slicked back exposing a large forehead. Above his lip was a mustache that looked penciled in.

"Cora, this is Giovanni. We met in Venice. He helped me order coffee and a scone," she said, giggling like a schoolgirl.

He took her hand and held it against his lips as if it were a treat waiting to be devoured.

"Isn't he just adorable?"

"Bellisimo," he repeated. With neither of them paying any attention to Cora, she left them in the kitchen, hoping Miss Lillian would get back to slicing the cake.

"Mama . . . Mama," Cora felt a slight nudging of her arm. Memphis was standing over her. She'd fallen asleep on the sofa in the midst of reading sympathy cards and trying to organize the plants and flowers that overran the living room. For every plant she'd managed to give away, someone walked through her doors with another one.

"It's late. You should go to bed. I'll help you with this in the morning," Memphis said, looking tired and worn herself. Cora knew this was the hour when death had its greatest sting—when the house was still and empty. But she felt at peace with the finality. In some ways, Robert Earl had been dead in Cora's heart for years. Some wounds couldn't be healed. But she'd honored her vows as best she could and had seen things through 'til death did them part.

"You go on to bed, I'm okay. I'm just going to finish up these last few," she told Memphis.

Memphis let out an extended yawn, kissed Cora, and started toward her old bedroom and then turned back. "I almost forgot," she said, groggily reaching into the deep pocket of her robe and pulling out a card Madison left with her before jetting out of the house to catch the red-eye back to DC

"I just hate having to rush off like this," Madison had said, talking as fast as her life was moving and throwing her things into her overnight bag. She was working for an up and coming young candidate for state senate who had been invited to speak at the Democratic National Convention. She had two days to help him finalize his speech. "I'll be in New York soon. We'll get together. I promise," she said, giving Memphis a quick but tight embrace. "Love you. And my parents send their condolences as well," she said, handing her the card.

Cora waited until she heard Memphis close her bedroom door before she opened the card. She recognized Thurston's writing.

Dearest Cora,

I am deeply sorry about the unexpected passing of your husband. I am even more sorry that it has taken this occasion for me to write to you, although I suspect that was for the best. While I only had the pleasure of meeting your husband that one day at the girls' graduation, I hope he filled your days with more joys than sorrows.

Memphis is proving to be an excellent young doctor. I truly enjoy having her in my office and the patients have really taken to her. You have raised an exceptional young woman and I see so much of you in her each day, so much so that sometimes it pains me to realize all that I so easily let go.

Nevertheless, I will not go on rambling. I simply pray you know that you have and always will be in my thoughts.

Love,
Thurston

She read the card again before putting it in the stack with the rest and going to bed.

Chapter 23

Being confident in this very thing, that He who has begun this good work in you will complete it until the day of Jesus Christ.

—Philippians 1:6

"Your home is lovely," Harriet said politely, eyeing the gifts lined along the living room wall and deciding whether to sit on the forest green and gold sofa. Memphis pleaded with Cora to remove the thick plastic lining she used to protect it from wear and tear. Instead, Cora tucked the edges in tighter to keep pieces from sticking to her guests. In the ten years their daughters had been friends, Harriet and Thurston had never been to Cora's home. Thurston had only seen the leaning wooden shell of a house in Black

Bottom, where they'd secretly kissed good night. Cora was certain her neighbors were peering from their windows to see who had emerged from the powder blue Mercury Cougar, a driver standing at attention.

"It's not much, but it's home," Cora said graciously, knowing her small cottage house was of no comparison to the French-decorated estate in all the photos Memphis had sent home of her frolicking in Madison's bedroom or enjoying a picnic in their backyard gazebo.

Harriet had only agreed to stop by the house at Madison's insistence. She had tried to convince Madison to stay at the hotel with her and Thurston, but as Memphis's maid of honor, she planned to spend one last night as single women with her best friend. They had already dashed off to Memphis's room squealing like schoolgirls.

"We'll be leaving for the church shortly for rehearsal," Cora called after them as she shuffled off to the kitchen.

Opting for a bubble bath and glass of wine over rubbery chicken and sugary punch, Harriet took the opportunity to make her escape.

"You and Madison are in the wedding party. There's no need for me to attend the rehearsal. I'll send the driver back for you," she whispered before slipping out the door.

Thurston settled in comfortably, inspecting family photos displayed on an end table. One in particular caught his eye. It was of a young Memphis, sitting on Cora's lap. Thurston guessed she was about three years old. He held the frame in his hand, trying to conceal a smile as Cora came back carrying a small tray of coffee. She searched the room for Harriet.

"She headed to the hotel. It was a long flight and she wants to be refreshed for tomorrow," Thurston said spontaneously, accustomed to covering for Harriet's moods and disappearances when she had grown bored or disinterested in present company.

"We can't thank you enough for agreeing to

walk Memphis down the aisle," she said, offering him a cup. Their hands slid past each other as she took the picture from him. She originally objected when Memphis suggested Thurston.

"Your Uncle Bo or Sadiqq would be more appropriate," she advised. But Bo complained about back trouble, and Memphis thought Sadiqq was too young. She didn't want to be walked down the aisle by someone who barely looked like he was out of his teens. And so Thurston it was, ready to do any and everything that was asked of him.

"It's my honor," he said, watching as Cora carefully put the picture back in its assigned spot on the table.

The wedding party milled around the sanctuary, waiting for the wedding coordinator to finish barking orders and sending them through an endless repetition of practicing the processional.

"I need the father and mother of the bride," she

yelled over the chatter. Cora and Thurston hesitated.

"Now! Please," she called again. As they stood in front of her, she looped Thurston's arm and guided Cora's through it, and then showed them how to march rhythmically behind the wedding party. Before they could get to the back of the church, Cora could see all of Memphis's bridesmaids gawking over a limousine.

"I have to take Mama home," Memphis protested as they tried to shove her in the car. Madison sprinted over to Thurston, and Cora instantly untangled herself.

"*Daddy!*" Madison said with a childlike plea. He knew what she wanted him to do and he was all too happy to oblige.

"I'll see to it that Miss Cora gets home safely," he said, offering a casual smile.

The tea kettle let out a high-pitched whistle. Cora brought tea, lemon, and honey to the table. Miss Lillian had finally gotten Cora to enjoy hot tea. She offered Thurston a piece of cake leftover from the rehearsal dinner. They didn't talk much on the ride home, and Cora expected him to say goodbye from the car, but he'd walked her to the door, so she felt the pull to invite him in.

"Who could have imagined I'd be walking Memphis down the aisle one day," he said, with an air of unexpected pride.

"Yes, who could have imagined," she said, swirling a spoon of honey into her cup. "I wish Robert Earl were here to see this day," she added, surprised that he was crossing her mind so much lately.

"Harriet hopes Memphis's wedding will put some fire under Madison to settle down soon. She's eager to plan the wedding of the decade," he said, managing a laugh.

"I'm sure it won't be long before you're walking *your* daughter down the aisle one day," Cora said with an undertone of sharpness in her voice.

She abruptly collected the dishes and walked to the sink dunking her hands into the cool sudsy water.

Thurston rose from the table and stood behind her pressing his chest into her back. Cora could feel his breath on her hair.

"Cora," he said softly, as if to keep the walls from hearing. "I can't undo anything that's happened, but I hope you know that I loved you."

As if pulled by an invisible force, Cora's head fell back onto his chest and she listened to his heartbeat. He folded his arms around her shoulders and instinctively she placed her arms over his. They stood silently, eyes closed, water dripping down their sleeves, catching the other's breath. For a few seconds, he was hers and she was his. The bong of the grandfather clock in her living room startled them both.

"You should go," Cora said solemnly, loosening herself from his grip and allowing him to show himself out.

Memphis slipped in under the covers, pressing into Cora's back and lobbing her feet on top of hers the way she did when she was little and seeking Cora's protection from an oncoming storm.

"Mama, are you awake?" she asked, as if her cold feet hadn't interrupted her sleep.

"Uh huh," Cora answered. She hadn't fallen into a deep sleep yet. Thurston and the business of the day ahead were weighing too heavily on her mind. And she could hear Madison already snoring in the next room.

"I really love you a lot," she yawned, her breath smelling of strawberries and sweet liquor.

"I love you too, baby."

Memphis giggled drunkenly, and Cora was glad the wedding wasn't until the evening, giving her time to sober up.

"This time tomorrow I'll be a married woman."

"Yes, yes, you will."

"I told Dr. Edwards he doesn't have to do all that father-daughter dance stuff, but he insisted." Memphis hiccupped. "Wasn't that nice?"

Cora was quiet.

"Mama?" Memphis said again, like the start of some childhood game.

"Yes, Memphis."

"Were you nervous when you and Daddy got married?"

Cora hadn't thought about her wedding day in years. She and Robert Earl stood in front of the pastor, encircled by Bo and Lil Sis. As they said their vows, Robert Earl's mother cried and Cora's father with his mouth left twisted and contorted from the stroke, grumbled under his breath. When it was over, they ate cake. "I was maybe a little nervous," Cora confessed.

"Well . . . I'm not nervous at all," she said with a bravado that reminded Cora of her first day of school.

"My little brave Memphis," Cora had said as her daughter hoisted the school bag onto her back and jetted off to the bus stop swinging her superhero lunch box.

"Mama?"

"Yes, Memphis." Cora's eyes were beginning to feel heavy and she tried to reposition herself in the bed to make room.

"When did you know you were in love with Daddy?"

Cora searched the databanks of her memory, trying to recall the moment she decided to love Robert Earl. When DC was nothing but a distant memory? When Thurston was no longer a possibility? When he took the time to pick her fresh turnip greens, help haul coal into the house or lift her father's ailing body? Maybe the night they cried together after burying RJ. She tried to find an answer—the right answer. But the soft slow hum of Memphis's breathing told her it didn't matter. She was asleep.

The deejay cued up a melodramatic love song, prompting starry-eyed couples to the dance floor. Madison sat restlessly watching and wishing she'd brought a date even if only for show. She also wished she could escape the pang of jealousy she felt from watching her father dance with Memphis. Madison knew she was adored by her father. But he admired Memphis, and Madison had grown tired of hearing about her come-up-from-nothing story, especially since it seemed she had everything now. She downed a glass of wine as Thurston proudly twirled Memphis in her wedding dress and handed her off to her new husband in exchange for Cora's hand.

A Stevie Wonder song was playing. They swayed back and forth, Cora watching the floor, careful not to step on Thurston's feet.

"I didn't know you could dance so well," Thurston commented, gripping her hand in his and leading their steps. His hands were soft, still not a callus or other sign of a hard day's labor.

When Cora was a girl, Black Bottom was filled with music on Friday nights. She and the other kids would jump around the dirt patch yards making up dances and imitating the adults. But it was Robert Earl who, over her objections, taught her to slow dance. The way he'd held her before they were married felt like a sin.

"It's been a while" she said, keeping count in her head.

"I probably haven't told you how beautiful you look tonight. If I didn't know better, I'd swear you were the bride's Lil Sis," he teased.

The last bars of "Ribbon in the Sky" faded out and Thurston pulled her closer, before they were blinded by a burst of red, yellow, and blue lights. A disco ball descended from the ceiling to the delight of the guests. Harriet pulled Thurston from Cora and they jumped into the forming conga line. The line snaked through the room with a smiling Memphis and her new husband grabbing people from their tables. The long, weaving centipede circled the ballroom before breaking into pieces on the dance floor. Thurston and Harriet bumped hips and worked to keep pace with the synchronized steps and turns of the rows of people starting to line dance. In the midst of a dip, Harriet lost her balance. Thurston scooped her up, sending them to the left while everyone else went to the right.

"Are we done trying to be young, Mrs. Edwards?" Thurston lightheartedly asked. They let out an exuberant laugh and then kissed, leaving Cora feeling like an intrusive voyeur.

"Grandma, let's dance," Sadiqq demanded, tugging eagerly at her arm.

"No baby, Grandma is done for the night. Go find yourself one of those pretty girls to dance with."

"Shoot, you're the prettiest one in this room," he said, flashing a boyish smile that looked more like RJ every day.

"Go on, boy!" she laughed, shooing him away and inhaling the air of love and joy around her.

Chapter 24

Members of the congregation were starting to trickle into the church. When Sadiqq accepted the call from God to preach, he hadn't expected his first assignment to be a small wood-frame church hidden from the main highway in a part of Tennessee he hadn't known even existed. He also hadn't expected to stay there for ten years.

The sparse sanctuary always looked bigger before mothers with restless children and seniors with canes and walkers squeezed into the oak pews.

The cries for a bigger sanctuary couldn't go ignored much longer. He'd resisted picturesque stained-glass windows, upgraded lighting, and an orchestra pit for the musicians, calling them a distraction. The most ornate thing in the church was the oversized chair behind the pulpit, reserved for Sadiqq. One of the deacons proudly told the story of how his great-great-grandfather chopped down his own tree and carved the chair for the church's first pastor over 100 years ago. Sadiqq rarely sat in it, choosing instead to walk among the people as he delivered his messages. Pacing briskly back and forth among the pews, he often laid hands on eager parishioners, making them feel as though he were talking directly to them. At times, he was sure God had given him a message specifically for someone in the congregation.

"I don't know who you are or what you're going through, but God does" he often started, his voice rising and falling as the spirit of God convicted him. His charismatic approach drew people, black and white, rich and poor, and from neighboring counties, to the little church that now hosted three services each Sunday. The local radio station gave him a fifteen-minute segment on Wednesday afternoons. "What time is it?" he asked, opening his broadcast. "Midweek spiritual tune-up time," a pre-recorded voice would answer back excitedly before he'd dive into prayer and a quick message. He had earned a reputation for being a servant pastor, risking confrontations with violent drunk husbands as he shuttled abused women and children to unnamed shelters; delivering meals to the forgotten few who spent their days and nights on wandering the streets talking to themselves, and standing in court, vouching for remorseful young men seeking mercy from the court and God for stealing a car or some other ill-conceived juvenile crime.

But it was the local farmers who turned him into a hero.

Incensed over a proposed highway expansion that would slice most of the land in half, a coalition of about twenty farmers planned a forceful resistance.

"We'll block every TDOT vehicle that tries to roll through here!" one farmer shouted during a meeting at the church.

"I've got enough cows to keep grazing across the whole area from now until January," another said.

Sadiqq listened, asked to do no more at the time than to open the church doors for the meeting. He felt their frustration and anger, but he knew mostly they were afraid—afraid of losing the only thing they knew and what they had worked so hard for. He also knew, twenty nameless farmers could be easily crushed into submission.

"You'll have their attention for a while, but then what?" he finally spoke up. "The governor will get a court order to have you and your cows moved, and the highway will go up."

"Well, what do you suggest?" one farmer asked skeptically.

"Show them your worth."

They didn't seem to understand what he meant at first until he had each farmer write down how much money their farms had brought into the community.

"Now, don't just think about yourselves individually," he instructed, speaking with the same passion he brought to the pulpit on Sunday mornings. "Think about how many jobs you've given people, the other businesses that depend on you, like the tractor supply store or the butcher for those cattle. Think of the grocery stores around here that you help keep stocked."

The farmers started to murmur thoughtfully as Sadiqq passed paper and pens around the room.

"Build the highway, kill the economy," the farmers chanted as they marched to the state capital carrying a sign with $3 million written across it. They were trailed by a couple of reporters who had gotten wind of a caravan of tractors coming into downtown Nashville. Sadiqq had told them it would be a good visual effect and they threw him out front as the spokesperson when the reporters started ticking off questions.

"These hardworking men and women, some fourth generation farmers, help put food on tables all over Tennessee and give jobs to hundreds of people. They're $3 million strong for this state. They don't want to stop progress. They just want to see it happen the right way," he said.

He had the reporters' attention and the camera was fixated on him. He stepped closer to the cameraman and looked directly into the lens.

"Today it's these twenty little farmers. Tomorrow, it could be your land and your farm. We're calling on all of those with family-owned farms across the state to join us in this fight for what's right. Build the highway, kill the economy!" he shouted, as the group began shouting behind him.

They settled in, locking arms and preparing to sleep on the cold concrete steps for the night. Another news station had come to the scene now, panning a camera around the huddled group. "What is it you want?" a new reporter asked.

"We want to see the Governor and we're prepared to stay here as long as it takes until he agrees to talk to us," Sadiqq said.

State troopers and capital police stood watch over the group during the night. It was a skeleton crew, and clearly nobody expected them to be there more than a day or two. Sadiqq wasn't even sure how long the farmers would hold out. But as morning started to crack through the sky, a wave of cowboy hats and overalls descended on the capital. He could hear the chant growing stronger, "Build the highway, kill the economy!" By mid-morning, a line of tractors circled the capital with more than 100 men, women, and children standing together, encouraging passing motorists to honk their horns in support of Tennessee's farmers. They were on every news channel and Sadiqq was front and center preparing to address the press.

"We will wait with the patience of Job to be

heard. But we will stand as strong as David against Goliath," he said over the roaring applause of the crowd.

The next day, fifty more farmers came, and they got their meeting with the Governor, along with a seat at the table to discuss options. And before long it happened. Sadiqq couldn't remember who first pitched the idea of him running, but he ran for county commissioner and then mayor. He won both seats by a landslide. But tonight's meeting was about more than winning over a few thousand county voters. There was a much bigger prize at stake.

*****

"What's wrong?" the governor whispered as he tried to nibble the tip of Madison's ear as if that would force her surrender. It used to.

What's wrong? she asked, and then answered herself. *I'm in bed with my married boss, the state governor.* Madison rose silently and slipped back into the hotel bathrobe he'd taken off her and thrown on the floor when she came out of the shower. He sat up, frustrated, and lit a cigar—the only thing he smoked since giving up cigarettes during his campaign. He watched her go into the bathroom and close the door. The night was over before it had begun and he huffily grabbed his shorts.

"I'm going to my room," he pouted.

No reply.

Madison stared at her reflection in the mirror. Her face painted the gray color of shame that was probably invisible to those who didn't know about all her late nights with the governor or the trip to Canada years ago to take care of her problem. It would have been nice to be able to call Memphis. She ran her hand across her empty abdomen, remembering all she had lost.

"I can't support you in this," Memphis told her. Madison was too recognizable to have the procedure done in the States, especially in New York. It was the downside of being an A-lister. She had expected Memphis to understand.

"All of us don't have the perfect life you do," she steamed.

"You're not doing this because you want to," Memphis shot back. "You're doing it for him, and he doesn't care anything about you!"

Madison slammed down the phone.

"God, I promised no more, and I mean it," she said, tears rolling down her face.

The Governor frantically rummaged through a pile of papers on his desk looking for talking points and a list of people whose names he was supposed to know. The Conference of US Governors was starting in forty-five minutes and he had been elected to open the meeting, the significance of which was not lost on a man with his political ambitions. In the last twenty-five years every former governor from his state who opened one of these meetings went on to Congress or the Senate. Peers who like you enough to want to hear you at 8:00 a.m. could mean they were ready to see you on a much bigger stage.

"Where is Madison?!," he finally shouted.

"She checked out, sir," one of his aides nervously answered.

"What do you mean checked out?"

"She's left the hotel. She's gone."

The Governor had been trying to call her all morning after he couldn't get into the shared door between their rooms. He figured she was still in a mood and had locked it intentionally. But she'd never been later for work and wouldn't miss a speech this important. He called her again only to hear her voice message. *"Where are you? Call me now!"* he demanded.

By the fifth buzz, Madison turned the phone off completely. She didn't want to talk or read texts from anybody. Besides, she knew it was him. Once he took the time to calm down, he'd find the event notes she left for him along with her resignation scribbled on hotel letterhead. Her mind clear and with a peace she hadn't felt in a long time, she buried herself under the covers and went back to sleep.

A rooster was crowing. Seriously. Madison's eyes fluttered open. She'd forgotten what it was like to wake up naturally. No buzzing alarm clock. No Governor's cold leg brushing against her, struggling to get up before daylight. She lay in bed, staring at the ceiling. She hadn't been to the family's upstate New York home in a while. Now that her mother was gone, her father had secluded himself here, fishing and reading mostly.

"Pud, are you up?" her father asked as he lightly tapped on the door. He'd been calling her *Puddin'* since she was a little girl. Embarrassed by it as a teenager, he shortened it to *Pud*.

"Come on in, it's open," she said without hesitation.

"I'm just checking on you. You've been here a week now . . . and . . . well, you know I love having you here . . . but . . . well . . . I was just wondering what's going on?"

"Nothing, Daddy. I'm just on vacation," she said, putting on her PR face. The face she used a million times. The face that swore there was no story until she could figure out the right angle to pitch. He smiled delicately, deciding to leave it alone for now and tossed her the morning paper.

Somehow she'd resisted watching or reading the news, but seeing the paper awakened a familiar urge. She thumbed through the local section in search of the national news briefs. The unexpected death of a beloved US Senator should have drawn her attention, but instead she fixated on a short paragraph about a young Tennessee pastor announcing his bid for governor.

She hadn't expected to see the Governor's car in front of her grandfather's home. Or to find him laughing and sharing a piece of pie with the housekeeper when she walked inside.

"Miss Madison!" the housekeeper sprang to her feet. "Miss Madison, I'm sorry, your father isn't here and neither were you, and I had no idea the governor was coming, so I wanted to make him feel at home and . . .," she stammered trying to contain herself.

"It's okay, RosaLee," Madison assured. "One wouldn't expect the governor of our great state to just show up unannounced." She shot him a defying look.

"Well, if you'd be so kind," RosaLee handed her a camera. "Do you mind?"

Madison took the camera and RosaLee posed for a series of pictures while the Governor smiled charmingly—the way he had the first night Madison fell for his seductive kiss. When she thought they were done, RosaLee set the camera up to take a picture of the three of them. The governor stood between them, his arm around Madison's waist, a touch she hadn't felt in over a month. When they were done taking pictures, the housekeeper left them alone to stare at each other uncomfortably while she retreated to the kitchen to whip up a meal he insisted wasn't necessary.

"I waited as long as I could for you to come to your senses and get back to work," he finally said, his voice low but firm. "I can't believe you haven't returned any of my calls."

"What do you want?" she asked dejectedly.

"I take it you heard about Senator Gary? I'm running for his seat," he said proudly. She didn't seem surprised.

"What does this have to do with me?"

"Everything. I need you," he said moving closer to her.

Her body stiffened and he stopped. He looked at her—really looked at her for the first time in a long time. Her hair pulled back in a ponytail, no power suit, no make-up. He saw her youth and the innocence he'd preyed upon. He hadn't loved her—only the power that allowed him to have her. Looking at her like a fragile wilted flower, struggling to revive itself, he understood what he'd done. The words "I'm sorry" hung in his throat.

"Not like *that*. I promise," he said. His face softened and he stepped a few inches back. "Just come help me win this thing. Please."

*****

Miss Lillian knew a few things about politics, mainly that winning took a combination of luck, timing, and, most of all, money. Intelligence played only a small role, and unfortunately for Sadiqq, intelligence was the only thing he possessed an abundance of, at least until Miss Lillian got involved.

"Come in, ladies. Welcome," she said hustling them into the house. Her invitation had promised tea with the state's next great governor, but no mention of who it was. Her plan was simple. Feed them. Flatter them. Guilt them into digging into their purses.

"Don't worry, Cora. Even if they won't vote for him, they'll give a donation. It will make them feel better about themselves," Miss Lillian assured her.

She and Sadiqq stood in the kitchen, waiting

for Miss Lillian's cue to come out into the living room. Cora still felt uneasy. She'd spent years catering to Miss Lillian's friends. Being the help was comfortable, familiar. Convincing them to give money to her grandson's campaign was different. It required them to see her and Sadiqq.

"We need to pray," Cora said as she took his hand in hers and they bowed their heads together.

*****

Madison listened intently as the Governor droned on about the campaign and road to victory. She would never be the first lady of anything, but she could leave her mark on every sphere of the political arena if she wanted. And even though she didn't want to walk away from it all, for the first time in a long time, she knew that she could.

"If you want me on board, you've got to do something for me," she finally said.

He perked up, waiting for her demand.

"There's a young man in Tennessee running for

governor. I want you to help him fundraise. *And* I want you to endorse him when the time is right."

"And who is this man?" he asked curiously.

"His name is Sadiqq Jackson. He's a black man."

He almost toppled over in his chair. Thinking Madison was joking, he let out a little chuckle, but stopped himself, the sharp look on her face telling him she was serious.

"A black Southern Democrat. Some would say that's political suicide."

"And others would call it progressive for a future US Senator, with an eye toward the White House," she shot back. "Besides, Governor Wilder did it in Virginia. Why not Tennessee?"

"Listen, I really don't think a New York senate candidate would be much help to him. I'm a Yankee after all," he tried to reason.

"You can let me worry about that. Now, do you want me on board or not? If you want me, you'll help Sadiqq. That's the deal," she said, standing with her arms folded in the warrior stance that he knew all too well.

Madison was the best. She'd helped him go from city commissioner to mayor to governor. He needed her more than he cared to admit and whether she believed it or not, he'd felt something for her. And he knew he owed her something for her sacrifice.

"Help me get some solid preliminary poll numbers, and then we'll make some party appearances together. If he proves he can cut it, then we'll go from there."

Madison searched the governor's eyes. Whenever he was lying his eyes fluttered uncontrollably. She was the one who convinced him to trade his contact lenses for eyeglasses. He had gotten better at lying over the years, but not to her. She knew the real man versus the politician.

"Deal," she said triumphantly. He leaned in to hug her and then pulled back, graciously extending his hand.

*****

About one hundred people scattered themselves in the rows of empty metal folding chairs. Most had come out of curiosity and the promise of free food. Sadiqq pulled out a multicolored map of the state covered in thumb tacks marking must-win counties.

"If we get Davidson, Shelby, and Montgomery Counties, that gives us Nashville and Memphis, among other key towns. If we do that, I . . . we can win this thing," he reasoned with an energy and excitement that was unmatched by anyone else in the room except Cora and Memphis, who nodded and clapped at every other word.

"That's a big *if*," one man said from the back of the room. He stood up and looked Sadiqq over, inspecting his pressed khakis and the neatly rolled sleeves of his button-down Izod.

"You really think you got a chance at this, don't you," he said sarcastically.

"Yes. Yes, I do; and I hope everybody in this

room believes it, too."

The man wanted to laugh out loud, but he was afraid he'd choke on his donut.

"Well, good luck to you, brother," he said, walking toward the door.

"I don't need luck, *brother*; I need your vote."

"Thanks for the donut, man, but you can't win this," another man said, joining others who were also rising to leave. Sadiqq wanted to beg them to stay, but that seemed weak. Instead he tapped into his preacher's voice.

"Where is your faith?" he asked in an energized baritone that echoed throughout the room. The group stopped and looked at him, giving him a few seconds to say something profound. Instead, they heard a still, calm voice from the back of the room.

"He's right. You're a black man, a Democrat in a Republican stronghold. And you're named Sadiqq. You can't win."

There were a few quiet gasps and even more

chuckles.

"At least, not without me." Madison emerged from the back and joined Sadiqq up front.

"Now, if anybody here is interested in making history, I suggest you grab another donut and have a seat." She smiled sheepishly at Memphis who gave her a warm smile in return.

Madison worked like a tornado with legs. She spent three days in Nashville and four days in New York, spinning ideas for Sadiqq's campaign as well as the governor's.

"When do you sleep?" Memphis asked, bringing her a third cup of coffee.

"When the election is won," she said with an exhausted laugh. Sadiqq had a campaign headquarters, a campaign staff of about fifteen people spread throughout the major counties, and a decent war chest of funds, thanks in large part to Miss Lillian. But his real team was Cora, Memphis, and Madison, and they spent hours huddled in Cora's house, strategizing about everything Memphis decided was important.

"You need a slogan," she told Sadiqq, thoughtfully reviewing the notes she'd scribbled together on the redeye flight into town. "Why do you want to win? Why do you want to be the Governor?"

"I'm a proven man of the people."

"Too cliché," she said, dismissively.

Sadiqq rubbed his chin. After weeks of interviews, community speeches, and hand-shaking marathons at fish fries, he felt like he'd given the answer over and over again.

"I want to fix what's broken and make every county and every citizen of this state stronger—poor, rich, black, white, all of us together and stronger."

"Too wordy," she said, shooting down his canned comments.

Sadiqq was exasperated. This was the part of politics he'd grown to dislike—being put in a decorated package.

"I don't know what else to tell you, Miss Madison," he said, sighing. "You want some catch phrase, but I don't want to just put words out there, I want to get the job done. I want to actually do what I say I'm going to do."

Madison smiled for the first time.

"And that's what you'll be," she said. "The get-it-done governor. You won't just talk about it; you'll *be* about it."

Sadiqq let the idea settle in his head. There was a rhythm to it that didn't sound artificial. He looked to Cora who had been sitting quietly. She offered little advice during the campaign, but he knew when she felt something was wrong or right. She shifted slightly in her chair, looked to Madison and Memphis.

"Sadiqq Jackson, the get-it-done governor," she said with a soft approving smile.

"No, just Jackson," Memphis quickly corrected. "You won't be Governor Sadiqq, you'll be Governor Jackson. Get the voters used to saying it now."

The room agreed. Jackson . . . the get it done Governor was ready to be unveiled.

Madison titled her head trying to force her ear to her shoulder to stretch her neck. Less than a dozen precincts were left to report. She clutched the leather binder securing Sadiqq's victory speech. There was only one speech.

"If you're not in it to win, there's no point," she'd told Sadiqq, the day they met.

The idea seemed crazy eight months ago. A Southern state electing a black man, barely thirty years old for governor. A black democrat, no less, in a red state. People laughed and talked about his foolish naïveté behind his back. They laughed even harder at Cora who swore she'd gotten a vision from God.

"Before the good Lord shuts my eyes and takes me on to glory, it's gonna happen," she said of her grandson.

There was no more doubt when the room

exploded into cheers as the TV reporter announced the next governor of Tennessee. Hi-fives and hugs were exchanged as Sadiqq picked up Cora and gently twirled her around the packed hotel room. Soon, everyone was scrambling for position and going over the background staging for his victory speech that Madison handed him on his way out of the room.

Epilogue

I would have lost heart, unless I had believed that I would see the goodness of the Lord in the land of the living. Wait on the Lord; be of good courage, and He shall strengthen your heart; Wait I say on the Lord!
—*Psalm 27:13-14*

Cora stood at the foot of the long winding staircase. Her mind teased her seventy-two-year-old body that most days felt much older, daring her to attempt the climb to the master living quarters. It was the only part of the mansion she hadn't seen. Feeling the tension in her knees, maybe she never would. But she had at least four years to try.

God had smiled on the day with sun-kissed blue skies overtaking the usual cold gray of a Tennessee January. The city was covered in a sheath of unexpected winter warmth. An occasional bluster of wind served as the only reminder that it was in fact still winter for the crowd that had gathered below the capital to hear Sadiqq's inaugural speech. He spoke powerfully of unity and the future, stirring cheers and chants of "Got it done; Got it done!" as a play on his campaign slogan.

They were hustled from the stage and back to the mansion to get ready for the luncheon. Cora had barely eased into a chair before Sadiqq rushed in.

"Grandma, it's time to go," he said hurriedly. "The car is outside."

Cora gave him her hand, and he gently lifted her up. They walked to the car arm-in-arm with pride and excitement written across their faces, Sadiqq looking so much like RJ.

Three dark Lincoln Town cars, one with the state flag waving in front, wound slowly through downtown before cutting across Charlotte Avenue toward the plaza. One carried Memphis and her family. The other held Madison and the rest of Sadiqq's team. Cora rode with Sadiqq who waved at the crowds as they passed through each intersection where police officers and state troopers stood at attention. She wondered what the people in Black Bottom, many of whom were long dead, would think of her riding in such a fancy car. She imagined even Robert Earl would be proud and happy, and she stepped out of the car and into the hotel.

A Who's Who list of state dignitaries stood like tin soldiers in a store window, elbow to elbow, unwilling to give up even an inch of the territory each had carved out to ensure just the right position next to her grandson for the inaugural photo that would capture the historical moment few had believed would happen.

Cora felt like royalty as she was escorted to the head table. Sitting in the over-lit ballroom with everyone passing by, greeting her with respectful handshakes and discrete nods and winks that acknowledged her as the grandmother of the state's first African American governor, she was glad she'd allowed Memphis to fuss over her hair and makeup, even though she had initially protested what seemed like self-indulgent vanity for a woman her age. Still, there was another reason she wanted to look her best.

Synchronized bongs of xylophones signaled a dimming of the lights and start of lunch. Sadiqq moved coolly to the podium under a crescendo of extended applause as Thurston quietly slid into the empty seat next to Cora. They shared a knowing, satisfied smile as their hands met privately under the table.

About the Author

Cora's Crystal Stair is the second novel by Rita Roberts-Turner following her sold out debut *God's Daughters and Their Almost Happily Ever Afters*.

Her work was also featured in the 2018 nationally released anthology, *All The Women In My Family Sing*. Rita lives with her family in the Nashville, Tennessee area.

Acknowledgements

To all the nameless and faceless "Coras" who through faith, strength and courage lifted their families to incredible heights.